GHOST TREES OF KIAH

GHOST TREES OF KIAH

Hilary Wilde

CHIVERS

British Library Cataloguing in Publication Data available

This Large Print edition published by AudioGO Ltd, Bath, 2013.
Published by arrangement with the Author

U.K.   Hardcover   ISBN   978 1 4713 4002 4
U.K.   Softcover   ISBN   978 1 4713 4003 1

Printed and bound in Great Britain by
TJ International Ltd

CHAPTER ONE

The hotel was in Vaucluse, an exclusive and fashionable suburb of Sydney. As Jacqui West walked into the massive foyer, she glanced round her curiously. It was the first Australian hotel she'd been in.

The receptionist asked her in an uninterested and impersonal voice what she wanted. Jacqui gave her usual swift and unconsciously warm smile.

'I have an appointment with Mr. Hollington,' she said.

Immediately the manner of the girl with beehive-piled blonde hair changed. 'Certainly,' she said very politely. 'His suite is on the third floor. The elevator is over there.'

Jacqui eased herself through the groups of elegantly-dressed people. Eighteen years old, she had the curiosity of a five-year-old. She loved working out what made people 'tick'. Obviously Mr. Hollington was either a very important man, or very wealthy.

In her three days in Australia, Jacqui had already learned some vital points. First, that Australians tended to use American idioms rather than English; secondly, that the aristocracy of an Australian was governed by money, not by birth.

The carpet was soft, a deep blue.

Everywhere mirrors showed reflections of the same people, women with massive hats, blue, white, yellow and every imaginable mixture of colour. Men, sun-tanned, were clad in immaculately tailored thin suits. Voices and different accents were everywhere. This was not typical Australia, surely, Jacqui thought, hearing French, Portuguese and even Greek.

The elevator carried her up silently and without any sign of motion. She walked down the long corridor. A porter in uniform told her that Mr. Hollington's suite was round the corner.

Everything was very modern, very luxurious and very impersonal, Jacqui thought. She wondered why she didn't feel more nervous and knew that it was because she didn't really mind if she got the job or not! It was all the Dunns' idea, but if it fell through, she wasn't worried, for she could easily get a job.

She knocked on the door and a deep, rather impatient voice told her to 'Come in'.

Jacqui went in. She blinked for a moment. It was an enormous, lofty room with the whole of one wall made of glass. The sun shone through it, this excitingly lovely sun that seemed to warm every inch of her body. For a moment the glare stopped her from seeing properly and she hesitated.

'Please come in and close the door,' the deep voice said. 'Don't look so scared. I'm not going to eat you.'

2

Jacqui blinked again, obediently closed the door, moved forward and, as her eyes adjusted to the bright light, saw the man who had just risen from behind a very beautiful sandalwood desk.

He was a big, broad-shouldered man with hair so fair and so obviously sun-bleached that it was almost white.

'I'm sorry,' Jacqui apologised easily. 'It was the brightness of the sunshine. I couldn't see anything for a moment,' she smiled. 'I'm not scared.'

He smiled as well. His face seemed to relax, to lose the look of stern self-discipline it wore when he was serious.

'I'm so glad.' He turned and pressed a bell. 'I'm just going to have some coffee. Will you join me? It's easier to talk when we can relax.'

'I'd love some,' Jacqui said.

She was a tall girl, slim to an appearance of frailty—a deceptive appearance, though, for she was amazingly tough. She'd had to be! The short skirt of her lime green shantung suit showed off her long slender legs. The soft ruffles of her white silk blouse emphasised the long slender neck. Her face was not beautiful, yet in many ways it was lovely. Her hair was an ordinary brown, but in the sunshine there were chestnut glints, gleams of gold; it was cut short and she had a wavy fringe on her high forehead.

She sat down on the couch he indicated and

3

smiled at him, then looked round the luxurious room. There were oil paintings on the walls of strange fantastic shapes in crazy colour, the thick carpet was off-white. The deep armchairs were covered in satin, old-gold in colour.

Mr. Hollington pulled up a chair, turned it round and sat, straddled, his arms resting on the back of the chair as he faced her.

He glanced at the piece of paper in his hand. 'I've already interviewed fifteen applicants,' he said in his deep voice. 'You are the sixteenth.'

Impulsively Jacqui clapped her hands. 'Oh, good, seven is my lucky number.'

He looked puzzled. 'Seven?'

'Yes, you see, sixteen adds up to seven. Six and one make seven.'

He looked as if he was trying not to smile. 'I see that, but I'm afraid the relevance escapes me.'

'Don't you know anything about numerology?' Jacqui sounded shocked. 'It's to do with the numbers in your name and your birthdate and your vibrations. Mine is seven and . . .'

'You want the job?'

The abrupt question stopped Jacqui speaking. She stared at him thoughtfully. What an unusual face he had, she thought. A mass of contradictions. Those unexpectedly dark eyes, half closed, almost—you might say—the eyes of a dreamer. Yet he had a square chin, a firm mouth and the voice of a man used to issuing commands.

'I'm not sure if I do want the job or not,' she said with her usual truthfulness.

The waiter wheeled in a trolley with coffee. Jacqui jumped up. 'Shall I be mother?' she asked easily.

'Please . . .' He also stood up, towering above her although she was a tall girl. He took the cup and saucer she gave him and went and sat down in an easy chair. 'If you're not sure you want the job, why apply for it?'

'It was really the Dunns,' Jacqui explained, carefully carrying her cup and saucer and putting it on a small table by the couch. She saw the faintly irritated look on his face. 'It's a long story.'

The man stretched out his legs, put his hands behind his head and smiled. 'I feel in the mood for a long story. Start from the beginning.'

'Well . . .' Jacqui half-closed her eyes, her pale skin making her look even more delicate and young than usual. 'It really all began when I was six years old. Both my parents died in a train smash. I went to an orphanage and was pretty miserable. My Aunt Elspeth, my father's elder sister, used to have me for the holidays. She lived in Caswatel, a small village in the south-west of England. I loved my holidays with her. Masses of cream, the cottage was part of a farm and the farmer's wife, a Mrs.

5

Croisey, was good to me. Then when I was about thirteen, I was ill. They thought it was polio, but it wasn't. Anyhow, the doctor advised country life, so I left the orphanage and lived with my aunt. It was very noble of her.'

'Noble?' There was a question in Mr. Hollington's voice.

Jacqui leaned forward, clasping her hands, her eyes wide as she went on. 'Oh yes. She was a spinster, you see, and her life was very regulated, and to have a noisy girl of thirteen dumped in her lap must have been very trying. That was the worst of it. She did her best . . .' Jacqui's voice broke slightly and she jumped to her feet. She went straight to the huge window and gazed out blindly.

'I tried to love her, but I couldn't,' she said over her shoulder. 'You see, she was a perfectionist—very ambitious. She taught music and did dressmaking. She hoped I'd be a good musician.'

'And you weren't?' His voice came from the room behind her.

The tears were still near, so she didn't turn round.

'I tried, very hard. I practised for hours and I began to hate music. Aunt Elspeth was so good herself. I could never hope to equal her. Then . . . well, I worked hard at school. She was proud of me, because I passed several A levels. I'm good at languages, I speak French,

6

Spanish, Italian and German. I'm also good at shorthand and typing...'

'Why then are you applying for the post of governess?'

She swung round. 'That's what I'm leading up to. Sorry I'm so slow about it. Four months ago, Aunt Elspeth died. There was no money for me, of course, and I had to get a job quickly. You see, I'd been helping Aunt Elspeth, as she was ill for some time, so I was giving music lessons at the schools nearby and...'

Jacqui sat down, drank her coffee, asked the quiet man if he would like another cup. He shook his head.

'Please, go on.'

She twisted her hands together, staring at her long fingers.

'I don't know what I'd have done without Mrs. Plaister. She's our Vicar's wife— quite old, got grown-up children, but she understands. She made me stay with them while I got over the shock, and ... and then she told me I ought to break away from the village and see the world while I was young. She said she'd give me introductions to friends in different parts of the world, and ... and here I am.'

'Surely you're very young to be travelling round the world alone?'

Jacqui looked startled. 'I'm eighteen, nearly nineteen. That's not young today, Mr.

7

Hollington. Lots of girls of my age have several children. No, it was the answer. You see, I'm what Mrs. Plaister calls a chameleon. That's a sort of lizard that changes colour according to his background.'

The man gave a half-smile. 'I am aware of that, Miss West. Please go on.'

'Well, the cottage wasn't my aunt's, but the furniture was and there were some really lovely antiques. Mrs. Plaister sold them for me and I had enough money for my return fare.'

'Return?'

Jacqui nodded. 'Yes, just in case I hated Australia and got homesick. It was an umbrella, Mrs. Plaister said. "Always take an umbrella and it will never rain," she told me. As I was saying, life in the village was very narrow. You saw the same people, discussed the same subjects. She said I should meet people. You see, like a chameleon I become like my background. In a village, I'm quiet and dull, in a city . . .'

'I wonder how you'd react to the Outback,' he said. 'It's a tough life.'

'I'm not afraid. If you lose both parents when you're so young, you learn to be tough.' She tilted her head, her left hand brushing back her hair. 'You have no choice. That's the best way to learn.'

He smiled. 'You certainly know all the answers. Go on. Mrs. Plaister gave you an introduction to someone in Sydney, I take it.'

8

'Yes.' Without realising what she was doing, Jacqui kicked off her shoes, tucked her feet under her and relaxed on the couch. 'They met me at the airport. They're just super people, really nice. They're rather upset, though, because he's been transferred to Tasmania and she's going to stay with her mother until he settles down and finds a house for them. She's going to Perth, but her mother's an invalid, so she can't take me. Then she suggested that as this was my chance to see Australia, I ought to stay here for, say, six months, and after that I could join them in Tasmania. She said it was a shame to be here and not see something of this country, and when she saw your advertisement, she said that the real Australia lay in the Outback, that a city was just a city anywhere in the world, so that's why I applied.'

'And why aren't you sure you want the job?' he asked quietly.

She looked at him. 'Frankly I'm not sure that I'd be much good as a governess. I love children, but . . .'

'You're little more than one yourself.'

She coloured. 'I'm nearly nineteen.'

'Actually,' he said thoughtfully, running his hand through his short blonde hair, 'I don't need a *governess*. I need someone who would be a companion. Maybe I'd better tell you the whole story in turn. I'm a bachelor and have a big station . . .' He paused and smiled. 'That's our word for a farm, not a railway station or a

9

bus depot.'

Jacqui laughed. 'There are so many different terms out here.'

'It's a young country and we're feeling our way,' he explained. 'To return to the matter in hand. I live alone. That is, I have an elderly cousin who housekeeps for me. I have several stations all over Australia and I get around quite a bit. Well, about three weeks ago, my sister came to visit me. I was away, and when I came back I found she'd left her two children with me. She didn't explain why, but apparently she had to go overseas immediately to join her husband. Cousin Adela and the children don't hit it off at all well. Life there is quite chaotic. I'm too busy to have time to sort out the trouble. Someone has to control those kids, if they are controllable, which I doubt. One's thirteen, the other ten. Both very spoilt and very anti-social, hating all adults.' He grinned. 'Not exactly an inviting picture, is it?'

'You said you'd interviewed fifteen people. Surely you found someone suitable?'

The man ran his hand through his hair again. 'How do you define the word 'suitable'? When I advertise for someone it's my principle to interview every applicant before making a decision. Always there are 'fors' and 'againsts'.'

'I expect there are more 'againsts' for me than 'fors',' Jacqui said. She was certain the job was not to be hers. In a strange way she was sorry for she felt troubled about the children.

10

Something must have happened to upset them to make them be so difficult. On the other hand, she wasn't sure she was the right person to handle 'difficult' children. Aunt Elspeth had always scolded her for not being more stern with the children she taught music to, but Jacqui's sympathies had always been with the children which made it very difficult.

'There are, quite many,' he agreed gravely. 'In the first place, you look delicate. We have dust storms, intense heat, sudden chilly nights, mosquitoes, flics, a horde of irritating allergies. It's often a lonely life. Our nearest neighbours are a hundred miles away. We have no doctor round the corner, though we can ask advice on the transceiver and the Flying Doctor comes out when it's urgent. A very different life from what you've led in England, sheltered. I think you would be wiser to seek a position in a city. On the other hand . . .'

'I'm not delicate,' Jacqui said indignantly, sitting upright, fumbling with her feet for her shoes. 'I'm tough. Look, Mr. Hollington, I can ride, drive a tractor or a Rover, swim, water-ski, sail a boat, milk a cow, look after pigs, handle dogs, play hockey . . .' she stopped for breath and saw that he was laughing.

She joined in and they laughed together for a moment, then Jacqui struggled to compose herself. 'I'm sorry. I didn't mean to shout at you, but honestly, Mr. Hollington, I am tough. On the other hand, I'm not sure that I'm the

11

right person for the job. If the children need a firm hand, I'm not good at that. I shall be on their side and . . .'

'Changing colour like a chameleon,' he said, with a half-smile.

'Yes.' She stood up. 'I do hope you find the right person, Mr. Hollington.'

He came to stand by her. 'You asked me for the 'againsts', but not for the 'fors'.'

Startled, she looked up at him. What a huge man he was! Surprisingly lean, but he had broad shoulders and was so tall.

'Are there any 'fors'?'

'Certainly. I think that perhaps your youth is what the children need. Someone nearer their generation. Look, Miss West, d'you know anyone in Sydney?'

'No, but I shall soon make friends.'

'What sort of job had you in mind? I mean, if you don't get this job?'

Jacqui shrugged. 'I haven't a clue, actually. I'm sure, though, I can get an office job. I'm told they can't get enough shorthand-typists.'

'Will you enjoy that sort of work?'

Jacqui gave a little grimace. 'I'll loathe it, but it needn't last for ever. I want to save up so that I can see something of this exciting country.'

'You like Australia?'

'What I've seen of it, yes.' She walked to the window. 'Just look at that!' she said.

It was indeed a beautiful view—the wide

12

harbour, the houses stacked either side, the hillsides of green trees and in the other direction the fairy-like structure of the Bridge and the strangely mystifying curves of the roof of the Opera House.

'I think that bridge is quite fantastic,' Jacqui said slowly. 'We drive over it to get to the Dunns' house in Cremorne. I had no idea it was so big or had so many lanes of traffic, plus a railway line.'

'They call it the Coat-hanger,' the man by her side said with a laugh. 'Have you come across the battle between the cities here yet? People from Melbourne sneer at the Coat-hanger bridge and Sydneyites tease the Melbourne folk by calling their river the 'upside-down river'.'

Jacqui turned instantly, her face alert. 'What a funny name. Why?'

'Well, the Yarra is very muddy, so they say it's been turned upside-down.'

They both laughed and then fell silent for a moment as a huge white liner moved majestically down the harbour, fussingly manoeuvred by the busy tugs. Some yachts went by, their sails pristine-white against the blue water, while small ferries cheerfully moved along.

'I adore this harbour. The Dunns are taking me to Manly this afternoon.'

'You'll enjoy that,' he said briskly. 'Now can you be ready to fly up the day after tomorrow with me?'

Absolutely amazed, Jacqui turned to look up at him. His squarish face was grave. 'You mean . . .?'

He nodded. 'I appreciate your hesitation about taking the job, so I suggest you come to us for a month. At the end of that period, you'll know if you like the life and I . . .'

'Will know if I can take it?' Jacqui said.

He nodded. 'Of course.'

Still she hesitated. 'I . . . in six months?'

Again he nodded. 'I understand perfectly. You've made the position absolutely clear. This would never, under any circumstances, be a permanent job. It might even only last for a couple of months, until my sister returns, you see.' He glanced at his wrist watch. 'I'm afraid I must go. I have an appointment. May I give you a lift?'

'Thank you,' said Jacqui.

They went down in the elevator and out into the blinding sunshine.

'You have dark glasses, of course,' Mr. Hollington said, as the green-uniformed chauffeur hastened to open the door of the long cream car.

'Of course, and I need them,' Jacqui said, fumbling in her handbag as she sat down by the man's side, pulling out the glasses and putting them on, smiling up at him.

'Amazing how different people look in dark glasses,' he told her.

14

'Yes, and how different other people look to you, Mr. Hollington.'

'One thing, we don't go in for Misters and Misses here. My name is Alain.'

'Alan? Rather nice. Alan Hollington . . .' Jacqui repeated as the car ran smoothly through the traffic towards the city.

'No, not Alan but Alain. A.l.a.i.n,' he said patiently.

'How unusual!' Jacqui began counting aloud. 'That's a one and a three and a one and a nine and a five . . . that's a one. And Hollington . . .' She half-closed her eyes, murmuring as she worked out the numbers: 'That makes a four and with one that's five.' She opened her eyes and smiled at her companion. 'You're a five. Isn't that wonderful? A marvellous number!'

The car was slowing down outside an enormous block of offices that seemed to be made entirely of glass. Alain Hollington glanced at the piece of paper he'd taken from his pocket and spoke to the chauffeur, who opened the car door for him and stood waiting. Then Alain turned back to the girl who was preparing to follow him.

'Ruggles will drive you home, Jacqui. We'll pick you up the day after tomorrow at nine a.m. You'll be ready?'

'Thanks. Of course I will,' said Jacqui, but she waited until he had vanished into the building out of sight, and Ruggles the chauffeur was neatly manoeuvring the car into the traffic, before she said the word aloud: 'Alain. Alain. Maybe he's got a Welsh or Norwegian ancestor. Alain . . .'

She sat back contentedly, enjoying the swift passage over the harbour, the drive through amazingly narrow lanes with stone walls on one side covered with ivy, with glimpses of the blue water and gardens ablaze with colour.

The Dunns had a small house overlooking Mosman Harbour with the Zoo on the opposite bank. Kay opened the front door as the great cream car drew up and Ruggles leapt out, opening the car door for Jacqui.

He was a tall thin man with leathery skin and very blue eyes. Now he grinned. 'Hope you know what you've taken on, miss,' he said cheerfully. 'Them kids is quite a handful.'

Jacqui laughed. 'I can imagine! Do . . .' she hesitated. 'Will you be flying up with us?'

'Bet your sweet life I will, miss. I go everywhere with the boss. We've got cars parked in every city. You're going to find it a very different life.'

She laughed again. 'Too right I am!' she said, and they both laughed. 'But an exciting one, I think.'

'Depends what you mean by excitement,' he said with an odd look, and then got into the car and drove away.

Kay Dunn, short, plump and with red hair and her cheeks flushed, her eyes bright as

16

she waited in the doorway, greeted Jacqui excitedly. 'You got the job?'

'Yes, to my surprise,' Jacqui agreed as they went into the hall.

'Goody! What's the salary?'

Jacqui stared at her. 'Oh no . . . he must think I'm dumb!' she said, beginning to laugh. 'I forgot to ask!'

CHAPTER TWO

Ruggles called for Jacqui promptly at nine o'clock. She was waiting and felt vaguely disappointed when she saw that Ruggles was alone. Kay Dunn gave her an impulsive hug.

'If you're not happy, Jacqui,' she said, 'don't stick it out. I'll be in Tasmania just as soon as Peter can find somewhere for us to live, and you'll always be welcome.'

The knowledge warmed Jacqui as she sat alone in the back of the huge car, being whisked through the traffic out to the airport.

Ruggles was not in a talkative mood. His leathery face was sullen as if he was annoyed about something, so Jacqui picked up her cue and was equally quiet. He carried her two suitcases inside and then said he'd see her later.

'I'm on the same plane, but I must make a phone call. Here's your ticket. Hope you're a good sailor. If not . . .' He rummaged in an inner pocket of his dark suit—he was not in a chauffeur's uniform—and pulled out a package. 'The boss told me to give them to you, case you've a need of them.'

'Thanks. I hope I won't!'

He grinned, showing several toothless gaps. 'Happen you will nearer the end. Then it can be real rough. But not in this great giant. A phoney sort of flying, I say. Wait till we're in our own plane and then you'll see.'

Jacqui felt rather alone as she went through all the preliminaries, but luckily she was used to coping by herself, so it did not alarm her. But she could not help feeling as if she'd been snubbed. What was it Alain Hollington had said? 'We'll fly up . . .' We? But where was he?

With the others she walked across the heat-scorched tarmac to the huge plane waiting for them. She took the seat allotted to her and waited. Then she saw Alain Hollington as he came on with Ruggles, who had a seat near the end of the plane. As Alain passed down the aisle, he stopped and smiled at her.

'Everything under control?' he asked. 'I'll see you later.' He sat near the front of the plane and almost immediately opened his brief case and began to read letters and papers.

'Never stop working, some folks,' a stout woman who had just sat down by Jacqui's side said to her. 'Just look at him! Can't relax for a moment. I bet you he'll have ulcers before

18

long if he hasn't already got 'em.'

Jacqui smiled at the elderly woman who was uncomfortably fat, her cheeks flushed, her eyes slightly yellow. She was wearing a dark frock and an old-fashioned hat.

'I suppose he finds this a chance to be free of phone calls and visitors,' Jacqui said.

The woman snorted. 'Know who he is? One of the richest men in Australia. Too right he is! He don't look so happy, though, does he? What's the good of being wealthy if you can't be happy? That's what I say.'

Jacqui had a good view of Alain's profile. His face was grave, his mouth a firm line. He was obviously oblivious to his surroundings, lost in his work.

'I wouldn't say he looked unhappy,' Jacqui began.

The woman snorted. 'Maybe not, but then I wouldn't say he looked happy either, would you?'

There were the usual announcements and the little scurry that precludes the plane take-off.

The stout woman sighed. 'How I hate flying, but it has to be done. I just keep my eyes shut till we get there.' She settled herself comfortably, closed her eyes and gripped her hands together.

Jacqui felt relieved at the consequent silence, for her companion would eventually have asked questions and probably

19

commented on Jacqui's job!

Alain turned his head and glanced down the plane towards Jacqui. He smiled at her, and she smiled back, and the feeling of being snubbed vanished at once. She found she could think of a hundred reasons why they were sitting so far apart on the plane. The seats had probably almost certainly been booked days ago, before he had decided on the new 'governess'. He wouldn't have wanted to be booked to sit next to someone he had engaged and yet didn't like personally. Her cheeks were suddenly hot. Was she thinking that he liked her?

Yet he had been so charming to her that she was sure he didn't *dislike* her. She relaxed in her seat and realised they were off the ground, climbing slowly up into the clouds. How thoughtful of him to turn and smile just at that moment and to think of pills for her to take.

It was an uneventful flight and then they were disembarking, the passengers talking as they walked down the gangway. Out in the hot humid sunshine again, Jacqui hesitated, not sure what was the next move, and then Alain was by her side.

'We've time for a meal,' he said, 'and then we go in our own plane.'

'Your own plane?' Jacqui said as they walked across the tarmac. 'Oh yes, Ruggles did say something about it often being rough.'

Alain laughed. 'Ruggles would! He's a born

pessimist. Actually it can be pretty rough at times, but I don't think it will be today.'

The restaurant was big and bright and crowded, but a passage was somehow made for Alain Hollington and a reserved table found. On Kay Dunn's advice, Jacqui had worn a thin white dustcoat over her blue crimplene frock; now she pulled off the small pillbox hat and relaxed in the chair. Alain was wearing a tropical suit, light grey. He looked relaxed, too, as he smiled at her.

'What about a cold drink? Or does a gin and tonic appeal?'

Jacqui considered the question. 'Could I have a brandy and soda?' she asked, and saw the question in his eyes. 'I don't often drink, but Mrs. Plaister says brandy helps if you're sea-sick or worried. It's one . . .'

'Of her umbrellas?' he finished the sentence for her, and they both laughed. 'Of course.' He called a waiter and gave an order, then studied the menu. 'How about a crayfish cocktail, then grilled sole to start with?'

'It sounds lovely.' Jacqui looked around her. 'You know, these airport restaurants look the same everywhere.'

'Yes, your friend was right when she said a city is just a city; the same applies to airports. This isn't the real Australia. The Outback is . . .' he hesitated. 'Didn't your friends want to know something about me? After all, I might be kidnapping you.'

21

Jacqui's laughter rang out. 'Of course they knew all about you,' she said. 'You're famous.'

'Me?' Alain looked startled.

'Even the woman next to me on the plane told me you were one of the richest men in Australia.'

'Oh, that! That's just money. That's not fame. Now if I had discovered something, written a bestseller, it would be different.'

Jacqui laughed. 'Oh well, whatever you are, the Dunns made sure you were trustworthy.'

Alain looked amused. 'Well, that's nice to know. How did they find that out?'

'They phoned lots of people, and everyone says you're highly respected, trusted and . . .'

'Feared?' he supplied the word that she had hesitated about.

Now she looked at him thoughtfully. 'That's something I can't understand,' she told him. 'Why should anyone fear you?'

He shrugged his great shoulders. 'Because, I suppose, I have power. Money gives you power to sack men, to buy up businesses and cause men to be redundant. I'm a hard worker and expect my employees to work hard. You weren't afraid of me, were you? D'you know, of all the applicants I interviewed you were the only one completely at ease, relaxed and honest.'

'Was I?' Jacqui was startled. She brushed her hair back. 'Maybe because I had nothing to lose.' She saw the question in his eyes, so went on, 'You see, I didn't *have* to have the job. I mean, I'm trained and know I can always get a job anywhere. I wasn't even sure I wanted the job, so I wasn't worried about not getting it. In addition, I don't think you really fear anyone unless they can hurt you. Or you're afraid lest you'll disappoint them or let them down.'

'You constantly stress this fear of letting someone down. I imagine you're thinking of your aunt?' Alain's voice was quiet, his eyes thoughtful. 'I can't imagine you letting her down. What gives you this guilt complex about her?'

Jacqui began to play with a fork, avoiding his eyes. 'Well, it's rather difficult. You see, no one ever loved my aunt—not even her parents or my father, nor her pupils. And she hadn't many friends. She was self-sufficient, I think that's the word. But only on the surface.' Jacqui lifted her head and stared at the man opposite her, her hazel eyes filled with compassion.

'Quite by chance I learned that she badly needed someone to love and someone to love her. I tried, I tried so very hard, but I just couldn't love her. She was kind, generous, but . . .'

'But . . .?' he asked quietly.

Jacqui looked down at the fork she had been twiddling. 'How can I explain? You can't love a lump of stone, something set and hard from years of hiding her feelings, so

23

that she can't ever hug you. Not even when you're a frightened child. Someone who is so controlled that she never cries, never shows excitement, pleasure, or praises you. How can you love someone who unintentionally makes you feel small, gives you the feeling that you've failed her, that she's trying to hide her disappointment? Yet she needed love.'

Jacqui looked up again, pushing back her hair. 'She was so kind, so good to me, so generous, but . . . but I just couldn't love her.'

'Perhaps you were wrong and she didn't need love,' Alain Hollington said, his voice strangely hard. 'It isn't everyone who wants to get involved with love—an emotion hard to control and full of pain. Perhaps she liked the safety of being unloved and unloving. Noone could hurt her, then. You could have been wrong.'

'I wish I could believe I was. I wish I could believe that she was happy, with her music and her home . . . but there was something about her that was so tragically sad. She had nothing and no one, not even a dog or a canary. Only me. And I let her down.'

He frowned. It was the first time she'd seen him frown, and it startled her, for it was as if a cloud had come down over his face.

'Why are you so sure you let her down? If she found it hard to express her feelings, don't you think that perhaps she *was* proud of you but found it impossible to put it into words?

You see, Jacqui, in a way I can understand how you feel. My parents were like that. My mother still is. She lives in Vaucluse but is a semi-invalid. She would be shocked if I failed to work hard and make a success of my life. But she can't praise me; she has never told me she loved me. She pecks my cheeks. She's like your Aunt Elspeth. Yet I've heard from other people that she *is* proud of me, that in fact she talks about me all the time.' He smiled wryly. 'In my family it's always been considered a sign of weakness to show emotion of any sort.'

He smiled suddenly and looked around. 'I'm getting hungry, what about you?'

'Yes, I'm hungry too,' Jacqui agreed. She looked at the man opposite her. He must be in his thirties, but he wasn't going grey yet. She wondered what it must be like to be thirty. It was very exciting being nearly nineteen with the whole world your oyster. As Mrs. Plaister had said, with Jacqui's training she could see the whole world.

'How I envy you, my dear child! Make the most of your chances. One day you'll meet Mr. Right, then you'll settle down in a semi-detached in suburbia, have a family and never save the money or have the freedom to travel. Make the most of it now. Many unhappy marriages are due to the wives feeling they've been thwarted, married before they had any real fun and resented it. Have your fun now and you'll never feel resentful.'

The waiter came quickly and they ate the delicious meal. Finally after ice-cream and strawberries they had coffee, then Alain glanced at his watch. 'I expect you'd like to go and powder your nose. I'll meet you in the hall downstairs. Ruggles will have everything under control.'

'He told me he goes everywhere with you,' Jacqui said as she collected her things. 'It must be very expensive.'

Alain laughed. 'I equate expense with what it gives me. Ruggles is a good reliable driver, also an excellent mechanic, and a loyal employee. Taking Ruggles with me ensures that I have no troubles on the way, as he can cope with anything. I also have only one chauffeur, instead of having to pay part-time chauffeurs in the different cities where I keep cars ready for me.'

Jacqui stared at him. 'You must be frightfully rich.'

He smiled at her. 'Depends what you mean by 'frightfully', Jacqui. See you in ten minutes downstairs,' he said, and turned away.

Jacqui paid her penny, washed her hands, powdered her nose, made up her mouth, and frowned over her hair that was a bit wild. She had enjoyed the lunch, enjoyed even more the talk with Alain, and she felt pleasantly sleepy. She was glad she had got the job; now she looked forward to the weeks ahead of her, seeing the true Australia, living in the same house as Alain, who was friendly and easy to talk to.

Ruggles and Alain were waiting for her. Soon she found herself climbing into a plane that could take half a dozen people. Alain was opening his briefcase, prepared to read. The pilot was in his place and the plane took off.

It was very different flying in this small plane from the huge plane before. The small plane often dropped suddenly and then soared aloft. Alain seemed engrossed in his papers. Jacqui sat very still. Ruggles was also reading—a murder story. Jacqui looked down on the ground so far below. It seemed very vast—just a plain with no trees or hills or lakes, just brown grass. They were probably suffering from a drought, she thought sleepily, and yawned. Out here . . . she'd heard . . . often for . . . for . . . years.

'Wake up, Miss Jacqui!' It was Ruggles' voice, Ruggles' hand shaking her gently.

Jacqui jerked herself awake, blinking, gingerly moving her head, as she had a crick in her neck. Now the plane was coming down, going in circles over a group of buildings.

'That's Kiah,' Alain Hollington told her. 'The word is aboriginal and means Beautiful.'

'It looks like a small town,' Jacqui commented.

'It has to be pretty big. There's the homestead . . . then there's my small house . . . and on the other side you can see buildings.

27

That's where the staff live, the jackeroos . . . that's boys who come to work to learn the ropes, and the mechanics. Right at the back, past that clump of trees, is a township where the abos live.'

The plane came down on a long runway. Men came running and Jacqui could see a big hangar, several planes parked, cars. Then she saw a crowd of aborigines who had grouped to watch, small black children holding on to their mothers' skirts.

'Well, here we are,' said Alain.

His voice sounded different. Jacqui glanced at him, but his face hadn't changed. Perhaps his mouth had hardened. 'Look after Miss Jacqui, Ruggles. I want a word with Abbott, but I'll go with Miss Jacqui to the homestead.' He turned away as he spoke and Jacqui was left with Ruggles, who led her to the doubtful shelter of the hangar.

It was scorchingly hot. Even as she walked, the flies came to greet her, crawling over her face. She lifted her hand to brush them off. As fast as she did so, more flies came. She looked ahead of her. There was just nothing. No hills, no trees, just flat ground stretching away as far as the eye could see. She turned to look at the homestead which was some two hundred yards away. Ruggles led her to a waiting car and sat behind the wheel, silently and with patience.

Jacqui looked at the buildings. And this was a farm! It was so completely different from the farms she'd known in England that she found it hard to believe. In the distance she saw a cloud of dust and the vague outlines of cattle. Nearer the house were several big dogs, golden brown with short tails and pricked ears. No sign of welcome. The children had not run over to meet their uncle, she thought—and at that moment Alain joined her.

'Sorry to keep you waiting,' he said curtly. He looked at her, but she saw he didn't see her. 'Trouble with Partridges, I hear, Ruggles,' he said to the leathery-skinned man's back.

'When isn't there?' Ruggles asked over his shoulder, as he began to drive.

'Well, it's time he snapped out of it,' Alain said curtly. 'I'll have a chat with him.'

Jacqui, sitting silently by his side, was startled. This was an Alain Hollington she had not met. She was beginning to understand why Kay Dunn had been told people feared Alain. Jacqui knew that she would rather not be in trouble with Alain. He was like her Aunt Elspeth, a perfectionist.

*   *   *

As Ruggles drove the car the few hundred yards to the single-storied homestead, Jacqui was mainly conscious of the heat, the flies that crawled over her face, the glare that made her head throb, and she had to battle against the sleepiness that kept creeping up on her.

29

This was worrying, for she was aware that Alain Hollington was looking at her. Probably he was already regretting the fact that he had chosen her, out of the sixteen applicants. He had said she was too young, and looked delicate!

She stared ahead, too tired to be really curious, at the house that was to be her home for the next few months. It was a large building, built in the shape of an L, with a screened verandah running all round it. Painted white, the bright colour of the flowering climbers made her eyes smart with their deep purple, the almost violent deep red flowers, and vivid yellow trumpets. She could see buildings on the far side, distant glimpses of horses in paddocks, something that looked like a windmill. Looking towards the horizon, something caught her attention and she stared at it fascinated.

It was simply a group of trees, but not just *ordinary* trees; there was something strange about them. They were tall, silvery white trees, without a leaf or a bud on them, with long branches dividing up into smaller branches and then into twigs, which looked absurdly like witches' fingers pointing accusingly or perhaps threateningly. She tried to smile at herself— what imagination she had! Yet the small group of white trees seemed to dominate the great expanse of yellow stubble.

'What are you looking at?' Alain asked.

Jacqui conquered a yawn as she looked at him. 'Those trees. I've never seen anything so fantastic.'

'Trees? Oh, those! The ghost trees.'

'Is that what you call them?'

He laughed. 'Some of us do. You'll see those all over the countryside. We had a bad fire here some few years back, came sweeping over. Luckily as it got near the homestead the wind changed and we were saved. But it destroyed most of the trees and bushes. That's all that's left.'

'You get bad fires here?'

'Sometimes. We've learned our lesson, now, and have wide fire strips and no trees near us.'

Even as Alain spoke the car stopped. Alain's hand was under her elbow lightly as they went up the six steps to the screened wire door. After the bright glare of the sunshine, the verandah was comparatively dark and Jacqui could only just make out the woman who rose slowly from a chair.

'You took long enough, Alain. The plane came in some time back,' she said querulously.

'Sorry, Cousin Adela, I had some business to attend to. This is Jacqui West, who's going to give you a hand with the kids.'

'She looks little more than a kid herself.'

Jacqui tried to smile, but everything went hazy as she made herself concentrate and look round her, seeing dimly how well-furnished the verandah was with comfortable-looking wicker chairs and tables and then at Cousin Adela who was staring at her, a small wiry-looking woman with snow-white hair brushed back from her forehead and twisted into a bun. Her skin was leathery-looking, like Ruggles', and her eyes a startling blue. She wore a thin dark blue dress, unfashionably long.

'How old is she?' she was demanding.

Jacqui found her voice. 'I'm nearly nineteen.' As she spoke, everything seemed to spin round her and she clutched at the nearest support. It happened to be Alain's arm, and he turned to her at once.

'You're tired, Jacqui. It's been quite a day. This is my cousin Adela, who looks after me so efficiently. Cousin Adela, would you show Jacqui her room and tell Sarah to make an omelette, a pot of tea, and take it to her. The child's exhausted.'

Cousin Adela gave a little snort. 'Child she is, too! That makes three of 'em.'

Alain ignored her and went on talking to Jacqui.

'You're just tired. You'll feel different after a good night's sleep.'

'I'm sorry . . .' she began.

'Nothing to be sorry about. Just one of those things. You'll feel all right tomorrow. See you later, Cousin Adela. By the way, where are the kids?'

Cousin Adela shrugged. 'How should I know? When I call 'em they don't answer.

32

They must be around somewhere. I wonder they didn't come when they heard the plane. Still, that's like 'em. No manners. Eat your food but can't even be polite. Come on!' she said gruffly, and took Jacqui's arm in her thin hard hand.

They walked down the long corridor. Cousin Adela opened a door and stood back. 'You've got your own shower. I'll send along some food in half an hour. 'Night,' she said curtly, and closed the door.

Jacqui stood leaning against the door for a moment, as she stared round her. Her suitcases were on a stand. Somehow she found energy enough to take a shower, partly unpack and slip into thin blue shortie pyjamas and collapse gratefully into bed.

The mattress was super! So were the pillows! But then everything was, here. It just showed what money could . . . do. She was half asleep when there came a knock on the door and a tall aboriginal woman stood there, a tray in hand. She had dark hair, a flashing smile in her dark face, and wore a pale blue dress and a stiffly starched apron.

'Thank you, Sarah,' said Jacqui, sitting up and taking the tray.

The food was delicious and Jacqui was surprised to find herself hungry. She finished it, then slipped out of bed and left the tray on the floor outside her door, got back into bed and closed her eyes.

33

Someone was shaking her when next she opened her eyes. She blinked. Cousin Adela was standing by her side, grumbling.

'Whatever next! Do they expect breakfast in bed these days? Well, if . . .'

Jacqui sat up. The quick movement sent daggers darting through her head and small whirls of vivid whiteness spinning before her eyes. 'I'm sorry. Is it morning? I must have overslept.'

'Is it morning? I'll say it's morning!' Cousin Adela began, but Jacqui was scrambling out of bed, racing for the small bathroom, which she reached just in time before being sick.

Cousin Adela was still there when Jacqui returned, feeling absurdly weak.

'I'm sorry, I . . .'

'Better get back into bed,' Cousin Adela said curtly. 'I'll take your temperature. Looks like you've got a fever.'

'I'm sorry . . .' Jacqui stammered.

'Look,' Cousin Adela turned half way to the door, 'just quit saying you're sorry, will you? I'm sorry too, but it can't be helped. Just get well fast, see?'

'Yes . . .' Jacqui began, but the door had closed. Now why had this to happen? She asked herself miserably. Just when she wanted to prove to Alain that she was not delicate! Poor Cousin Adela! Instead of the new governess taking the children off her, Cousin Adela now had a patient to nurse!

An hour later, Cousin Adela brought her some tablets. She'd taken Jacqui's temperature, said nothing, left her and later had sent Sarah with a glass of cool lemonade. Now she came back.

'I've been talking to Dr. Mullins,' Cousin Adela said abruptly. 'You're to stay in bed and take these pills. He thinks it's some bug you've picked up. Anyhow, if you're no better in two days, he'll be coming out to his clinic, anyhow. Now you take these tablets every three hours. He says not to eat anything, drink plenty and sleep.'

'Thank you very much. I'm . . .' Jacqui began, and stopped. She managed a smile. 'I'll try to get well quickly.'

Cousin Adela looked at her grimly, her eyes unfriendly.

'You'd better. More trouble than you're worth. I can't think what Alain was doing when he engaged a bit of a girl like you,' she grumbled as she left the room.

Jacqui took the tablets and lay down again, closing her eyes. As sleep took over, she found herself remembering some of the country people at home, how long they took to accept 'furriners', how hostile they always seemed to new people, yet how kind if anyone needed help. Poor Cousin Adela! She couldn't be blamed for being annoyed with the new 'governess', could she?

Two days passed and Jacqui slept most of

the time, but when she was awake she still had the feeling of nausea and utter exhaustion, while Cousin Adela and Sarah seemed to drift in and out of her bedroom.

Then she heard a plane roaring overhead. That must be the doctor, she thought. She sat up, trying to smooth down her ruffled hair, wondered if she had the energy to get out of bed to find a comb, and decided she had not. She heard Alain's voice in the corridor as the door opened.

'Yes, well, I guess she did look delicate right from the beginning, but I didn't expect this. What? Oh, yes, she flew out from England three days before . . . could have been four days, I'm not sure. Then we came up here.'

'Some people react like this when they've flown too far in too short a time,' a different voice said. A voice that had a slight hit of an Irish accent. 'Anyhow, I'll take a look at her.'

The door opened wider and a man stood there. He was short in comparison with Alain, who gave Jacqui a brief smile, lifted his hand, and walked away.

'Hi, there, I'm Dan Mullins,' the short man said. He had light brown hair, rather long and untidy. He wore khaki shorts and a matching shirt. 'Well, this is a fine way to start life in the Outback!'

He came to her side, his hand cool on her wrist. He asked her a few questions, took her blood pressure, sounded her heart, tapped her

36

knees, then he jerked a chair to sit by her side, smiling at her.

'Tough luck, starting out like this,' he said, his voice friendly. 'Did you feel ill on the way up? I mean, it can be pretty rough.'

'No. I just felt horribly sleepy. In the end, I did sleep most of the way.'

He nodded. 'And you felt all right when you got here?'

She hesitated. 'Well, not quite all right. You see, everything looked strange, as if something was whirling before my eyes so that I couldn't see properly. But I didn't feel sick, not till next day.'

Smiling, he patted her hand. 'Nothing to worry about. We'll soon have you up and about again. Though maybe you'd rather stay here.' He chuckled. She saw that he had green eyes. 'How're you getting on with the old dragon?'

'The old dragon?' Jacqui echoed.

Dan Mullins put back his head and laughed. 'Cousin Adela, I mean. We all call her the old dragon.'

'She's been very kind to me,' Jacqui said indignantly. 'I think that's horrid of you!'

Dan laughed again. 'Of course it is. I am horrid. No, seriously, Jacqui, she has the proverbial heart of gold, but it's so covered with bitterness and resentment that it rarely shows.'

'I don't blame her for being mad at me—

after all, I'm supposed to be here to help her.'

'Maybe you are helping her,' he said, and stood up. 'I'm going to give you an injection. Tomorrow you can get up for an hour, then four hours the next day, and so on. By the end of the week you'll be okay. Just watch out for the sun, Jacqui. It takes us Pommies a while to realise the strength of it here. Always wear a hat when you go out or you could be in real trouble.' He smiled at her. 'Once you've overcome this business everything'll look different, Jacqui. This is a great life and a grand people.'

Half way to the door he turned round. 'You're used to handling kids?'

She shrugged. 'I've taught music to children, but that's all.'

'Then may the good lord help you,' Dan Mullins said with a smile, 'for you're certainly going to need help ! 'Bye.' He went out of the room with a final wave of his hand, closing the door behind him.

*   *   *

As the doctor had prophesied, Jacqui made progress. Each day she felt stronger and the nausea vanished. At first her legs were shaky, but gradually she began to return to normal life.

If life in Australia could be called 'normal', she thought sometimes. Everything was so different—the sunshine, the glare, the heat, the humidity; the vastness of the flat distance, stretching away to vanish into a heat haze, the size of the 'station', which she still thought of as a 'farm' if she wasn't careful.

Those ghost trees she saw as she sat on the verandah, so tall, so alone. The people . . .

The Dunns had been English, so the Hollingtons were the first Australians she had really known. Cousin Adela was just as hostile, just as full of grumbles, just as difficult to help. As Jacqui grew stronger, she tried to see what she could do to make the wiry, energetic old woman accept her, but it seemed as if there was no way. If Jacqui went into the kitchen she was almost chased out of it.

'Too many people out here will get in the way,' Cousin Adela grumbled at her. 'You've been engaged to take charge of the kids, not to mess about with me. I'm not so old I can't manage, you know.'

It seemed impossible to placate her, so Jacqui decided to give time the chance to achieve the impossible, and kept out of the old woman's way as much as she could.

The children were even more difficult. They were silently hostile, which was harder to contend with because Jacqui could not discover why they refused to like her. On her first day up, she was sitting on the verandah in a very comfortable wicker chair, when Alain came up the steps, the children with him.

'Well, Jacqui, really feeling better?' he asked, standing before her, towering above her. His hair was wet with sweat, the khaki shorts and shirt he wore were crumpled. 'I wanted you to meet the kids. This is Sally.'

He had the children by the hand and pulled Sally forward. She glared at Jacqui silently, a lanky girl with straight dark hair, dark smouldering resentful eyes, and spots all over her face.

'Say "hullo," Sally,' Alain said, his voice exasperated.

'Hullo,' the girl said sullenly.

'And this is Gaynor,' Alain went on.

Jacqui stared at the boy. He looked about ten, almost pathetically thin, blond almost too pretty to be a boy, with a shy, mournful face. His eyes were wary, even perhaps fearful. He spoke without being pushed by his uncle.

'Hullo.'

'Hullo,' Jacqui said in turn.

'Jacqui is here to keep an eye on you both,' Alain said. 'And to keep you off your aunt's back.'

'She isn't our aunt,' said Sally. 'She's a second cousin twice removed.'

'That's as may be, but she prefers you to call her Aunt.'

Sally glared up at him. 'I don't get it, Uncle. You tell us not to tell fibs one moment and the next you tell us to lie and call her Auntie.'

Alain's mouth moved as if he was trying not

40

to smile.

'Look, Sally, Cousin Adela is used to being addressed respectfully. She feels you're too young to call her Adela or even Cousin Adela, so she wants you to call her Auntie. That's not lying, that's politeness. Now, be good children and don't let Jacqui get too tired or we'll have the doctor after us. I'm going to have a shower, so I'll leave you all to get acquainted.' He went through the swing door into the homestead, and Jacqui and the two children stared at one another.

'Won't you sit down?' asked Jacqui.

They obeyed. Another long silence.

'Have you had a governess before?' Jacqui asked.

'Of course we have. Often,' Sally said scornfully.

'Well,' Jacqui hesitated, 'would you mind telling me what they do? You see, I've never been a governess.'

She thought she saw a glint of interest in Sally's eyes, but it vanished at once.

'A governess is a nuisance,' Sally said. 'She stops you doing all the things you want to do, makes you go to bed when you're not sleepy and get up when you're tired, and eat food you hate and . . .' she paused for breath.

Jacqui was trying not to smile. 'Oh dear, have I got to be such a monster?' she said, and smiled. 'Well, there's one good thing, then, that I've just remembered. Your uncle didn't

41

engage me as a *governess* exactly, you know, he said a companion.'

'Companion?' Sally's voice was contemptuous. 'How can you be a companion? You're an oldie and a square.'

'I am not,' Jacqui pretended indignation. 'I'm only eighteen.'

Sally's eyes widened. 'Then you're still a teenager?'

'Yes.'

'When did you leave school?'

'Six months ago.'

'Did you go out and work?' Was there a little interest in Sally's questions? Jacqui wondered hopefully.

'No. I helped my aunt teach music.'

'You play the piano?' Gaynor spoke for the first time.

'Yes. Have you got a piano?'

'M'm, but it wants tuning,' Gaynor explained. 'I play the piano too.'

'I bet you don't like pop music,' said Sally. 'I bet you just play that classical stuff.'

'I'm afraid I'm not all that keen on classical stuff. I had too much of it at home. My aunt loathed pop music, so I used to listen to my transistor under the bedclothes when I was supposed to be asleep, at night.'

'You did?' Sally's face brightened. 'I . . .' She stopped speaking abruptly as the door opened and Alain stood there. His hair was wet from the shower, his shorts and shirt immaculately clean.

'Time to run along, kids,' he said. 'Jacqui mustn't overdo it. Another few days and she's yours full time.'

Sally opened her mouth, looked at Jacqui and closed it again. She stood up, glared at Gaynor. 'Come on,' she said curtly, and they went out.

Alain sat down and smiled at Jacqui.

'Well, were they real *enfants terribles?*'

'No, but Sally isn't exactly friendly, is she?' said Jacqui.

He shrugged. 'Been spoilt by their parents. I think they'd both be better off in boarding school.' He stood up. 'Glad you're feeling better, Jacqui.'

'I am sorry about it,' she began.

He smiled at her. 'Not your fault, Jacqui. Mullins says it was a kind of bug. Seems there's quite a lot of it about. He also thinks there was some emotional factor. I told him about your aunt's death and the sudden decision to come out here. You didn't mind?'

'Of course not. But it wasn't *hard* to decide to come out—I mean I haven't left anyone behind that really matters.' Her hand flew to her mouth with dismay. 'That's mean of me! Mrs. Plaister means a lot to me. She's been so kind.'

'The one with the umbrellas?' Alain asked with a smile. 'Anyhow, you'll soon be yourself again.' He walked out of the wire door and

43

left her.

The next day, the children had spent longer with her than before. They all sat on the verandah, trying to find something to talk about.

'You're English?' Sally asked abruptly. 'I suppose you despise us.'

Jacqui was really startled. 'I despise you? Why?'

'Because we're only Colonials . . . because our ancestors were convicts.'

'Convicts? But . . .' Jacqui began.

Sally sniffed. 'I wouldn't be English for all the tea in China. Fancy deporting all those poor wretched people out to a great barren land to starve!'

'Convicts!' Jacqui said again. 'The bell has rung, Sally. You're thinking of those dreadful years when people were deported for stealing a loaf of bread? They weren't real convicts, not real baddies. Why, I know a stone bridge in England that has a notice on it 'Trespassers will be deported'. I ask you! Deporting a trespasser for walking on a private bridge! No, that was a shocking time, but the convicts that were sent out here weren't really criminals.'

'You treated them like it and despised us ever since,' Sally said stubbornly.

'Look, Sally, it wasn't only Australia that got them. Masses of convicts were deported to the United States of America. You don't hear *them* talking about their convict ancestors.'

44

'No, because they broke free from the English. That's what we ought to do.'

'What's England like?' Gaynor asked suddenly. 'Is it like here?'

'Of course it isn't, stupid,' Sally told him. 'It's small and there's no grass or trees because everywhere there's houses and cars and trains. It's a very small island just packed with people, so there's no room to move . . .' She stopped speaking to stare at Jacqui, who was rocking with laughter. 'What's the joke?'

'Oh, Sally, I don't know who's told you about England, but they're so wrong. Of course England is small and it has a lot of people—fifty million. That's something like five times as many people as you have here. Of course there are lots of houses, but there's miles and miles of country, of lovely hills, downs we call them usually, of fields and woods and . . . parks. You should see the large number of parks in London. I've got some photos.' Jacqui stopped laughing. 'Look, I grant you that England is very small when compared with Australia,' she went on, 'but I promise you, Sally, it's not *all* houses and people. You can still move and breathe. It's a very ancient country, whereas yours is a new country, only a hundred and fifty years old or so, while England . . . why, you've surely heard of the Battle of Hastings in 1066, and that wasn't anywhere near the beginning of England.'

'I suppose that's why you despise us because we're a young country,' said Sally.

'But, Sally, what makes you think we despise you? If we did would so many people emigrate? Everyone thinks Australia is a wildly exciting country, a lovely country.'

'You like Australia?' Gaynor asked.

'I love what I've seen of it. I only had four days in Sydney, and since I've been up here I haven't seen much.'

'D'you like Sydney?' Gaynor asked. 'Granny lives there. Sometimes we go and stay with her.'

'Not often,' Sally butted in. 'She doesn't like children. I don't think she likes anyone much.'

'Oh, Sally, she's an invalid, isn't she? When we're young, we get on old people's nerves.'

'Mummy isn't young, but Granny says *she* gets on her nerves!' Sally said.

'Where d'you live?' Jacqui asked, to change the conversation.

Sally's face seemed to pucker. 'Where Daddy is. Come on, Gaynor, Jacqui mustn't get tired.' She gave Jacqui a quick glance. 'Bye!'

Jacqui sat still for a long time after the children had left her. Did all Australian people think the English despised them? Later that day she had the chance to ask Alain.

He laughed. 'Some think that. You see, Jacqui, Australia felt very cut off from the world, very isolated, left on her own. She

46

wasn't a wealthy country, in fact, she had a hard struggle after the First World War. In those days communications were not as they are today. Australians felt they'd been forgotten by Britain, that they weren't wanted. I don't think you'd find that belief today. Television, telephone, jet air flights have all brought us into the picture. Australia is battling still, but succeeding.'

'She's a strange girl, Sally,' Jacqui said thoughtfully. 'Something has upset her. I wonder what it is.'

Alain laughed. 'That's her affair, not ours. Don't start being your brother's keeper, Jacqui, or you'll get hurt.'

Jacqui showed her surprise. 'But Sally may need help.'

Alain looked at her thoughtfully. 'Jacqui, I know you have the best of intentions, but it doesn't always help the person you *want to* help, if you try to help them. Sometimes the person will be helped most if she or he is left to fight her own battles and overcome her own problems.' He smiled ruefully. 'I can see I'm not making things clear. Mind if I light my pipe?'

'Of course not.'

Jacqui tried to relax but realised she was sitting on the edge of her chair. Through the screens she could see the glaring sunshine, the great stretch of yellow dried grass that went into the distance, the starkly bare ghost trees.

47

'Look, Jacqui,' Alain, his pipe packed and lit, crossed his long legs and smiled at her, 'don't look so worried. The point is that Australians are independent people. They don't need cosseting and they often see an offer of help as a threat to their independence. They hate having to admit the *need* of help. It's a young country, the inhabitants are super-sensitive. They might even see your attempts to help them as interference.' He lifted his hand as she tried to speak.

'I know. You mean well. You don't have to tell me that. Remember, however, that you're young, naive and an idealist. But there's another side to this question of helping others. In your desire to help them, you may start delving into their problems and hurt them more than if you had left them to fight their own battles.'

Jacqui's face was unusually serious. 'I hadn't thought of that side of it.'

He smiled again. 'I know. That's what I said just now. You mean well.' He stretched out his legs and sighed. 'Life isn't straightforward, Jacqui. You've spent most of your life in a quiet country village where black was black and white was white, where people in trouble welcomed help and didn't resent it.'

'I can see that, but I don't see what this has to do with Sally.'

'Maybe not, but I'm afraid that if you start with Sally's problems, there'll be no end to

48

your helpfulness. I'm quite certain you're already worried about Cousin Adela and are wondering how you can help her to be happy.'

A red flush crawled over Jacqui's cheeks. 'Well . . .' she began.

Alain was smiling. 'See what I mean? The truth about Cousin Adela is that she enjoys moaning. What we out here call *wingeing*. As long as I can remember, she has grumbled. It's part of her. But it doesn't mean she's unhappy.'

'Dr. Mullins said she has a heart of gold if you could see it.'

'Dr. Mullins?' Alain's voice changed slightly. He sounded almost disapproving, but then he smiled. 'It doesn't do to believe everything that Danny Mullins says. He's got a big mouth and loves shooting it off. We call him the local gossip.'

'He said Cousin Adela was bitter and resentful.'

This time Alain did frown. 'I wish . . . Look, Jacqui, there are very few people in this world who don't believe they have reason to be resentful. Some overcome it, others revel in it. Cousin Adela has every reason to feel bitter and resentful, but that's her business, not yours. She's happier today than I've ever known her, so please leave her alone.' There was a faint tinge of impatience in his voice, but again he controlled it and smiled at her.

'What's really worrying me, Jacqui, is that

49

at some time or other you'll start working on me. Why is Alain a bachelor, your young, quick, anxious mind will ask! Maybe he's had a broken heart? Perhaps he's in love with someone who has rejected him? How can I help him . . .? Now, you'd do this with the best of intentions,' he went on, watching the slow blush cover her face, 'but I don't want you delving into my life. I'm a happy man, busy, enjoying my life. Because I'm single it doesn't mean . . .'

'I know, but. . .' Jacqui paused, uncomfortably aware that she was blushing again. 'It must be such a lonely life.'

Alain began to laugh. He stood up, his hand lightly on her shoulder. 'I assure you I haven't time to be lonely. You're so young, Jacqui. Just relax and enjoy life. You're a romantic and in time some handsome man will ride up on a white charger and carry you off to the sound of wedding bells, and you'll live happily ever after, but you're young now, and free, so just enjoy yourself. See you!' he finished abruptly, swung open the door and walked into the glaring sunshine.

Jacqui sat still, watching his tall, broad-shouldered figure as he walked towards the staff quarters. Was he right and she wrong? Was trying to help others a form of interference? If she was unhappy, would she welcome strangers trying to help her? Yet if there *was* something you could do to help

50

them, ought you just to sit back and look the other way? Wasn't that what Mrs. Plaister would call 'passing the buck'?

Thinking of Mrs. Plaister, Jacqui went to her room and got her writing pad. She had so much to tell Mrs. Plaister, who would enjoy reading it.

'I've always wanted to see Australia,' Mrs. Plaister had said, 'but there isn't much hope. Let me see it through your eyes.'

Leaning over the pad, pen poised in readiness, Jacqui did a quick think. How could she show Australia through her eyes?

In the first place, she could stress its vastness, which still staggered her. One thousand miles between cities. One thousand . . .!

Then the size of this station. Alain had told her once, but she had forgotten, but it went into something phenomenal, bigger than an English county.

In addition there was the mechanical side of this station. They had three planes. Apart from Alain's private plane that they had flown up in, they had two other planes for fertilising and spraying his citrus orchards down south. He kept the planes here, as this was where his mechanics lived, so they could service them. He also had a helicopter!

It was just staggering. He must be made of money. And yet he was friendly and understanding. How, Jacqui wondered, could anyone really be afraid of him?

CHAPTER THREE

Once Jacqui was well, things began to improve. Even grumbling Cousin Adela, although she showed no sign of friendship, at least showed less hostility—perhaps because Jacqui had taken over the children, supervising their lessons, their meals, their leisure hours.

The children too, had changed. Sally was still moody, often sullen, enjoying sarcastic remarks, but she was obviously accepting Jacqui's presence as something that had to be endured. Gaynor for all his shyness was the most friendly of the two, but then he was so different from his sister. Sally was a real tomboy, always off riding with one of the jackeroos, or watching the mechanics servicing the trucks or Land Rovers. Gaynor preferred to sit somewhere and read. Now he took Jacqui under his wing and on a tour of inspection.

'I just can't get over the size of it all,' Jacqui said as she and Gaynor walked past the large staff quarters, a long single-storied building with a dozen bedrooms, each with a shower, a huge dining room and a playroom, with billiards, darts and a small library.

Gaynor smiled. 'You're always saying that.'

Jacqui smiled back, 'And I'll go on saying it.'

On the other side of the L-shaped homestead, some fifty yards away, was a small building. Jacqui called it a bungalow, but Gaynor corrected her:

'That's also a house, a single-storied house, not a bungalow.'

She smiled and accepted it.

'It's Uncle Alain's,' Gaynor went on. 'We're not allowed there, ever. Not unless it's a 'mergency.' He smiled at Jacqui. 'Sometimes we don't see him for days, he eats and sleeps there, but since you've been here, we've seen him more.'

Behind the homestead was a circular lawn with beds of flowering shrubs, gorgeous white sweet-smelling flowers, others were deep red and yellow.

'Everything here is so colourful,' Jacqui said. 'It almost hurts my eyes.'

'You'll get used to it,' Gaynor told her wisely, looking up at her. He wore white shorts and matching shirt, while Jacqui was grateful that, in the mad rush before she left Sydney, Kay Dunn had taken her to David Jones' and made her buy half a dozen drip-dry batiste frocks, which were light and cool. Today she wore a green one and Cousin Adela, with a sour look, had lent her a big straw hat.

'Now don't you take that off,' she'd said sternly. 'I don't want you down with sunstroke.'

'I won't,' Jacqui promised.

Behind the circular garden was a tall

53

hedge of bougainvillea and, surprisingly, honeysuckle. The mixture of purple and sweet-smelling white flowers was both lovely and picturesque. Beyond that was the swimming pool and tennis court.

'D'you play tennis?' Jacqui asked.

Gaynor shook his head. 'I hate games. Sally does. So does Daddy.'

'Doesn't your mother . . .?' Jacqui began.

'No. I'm thirsty, let's go back,' said Gaynor, turning.

'All right.'

Jacqui had noticed several times that at any mention of his mother Gaynor seemed to clamp down, to almost retreat, his face going quite bleak. She began to wonder why—and stopped herself. Alain had warned her against being inquisitive!

The amazing luxury of the place for all its isolation also surprised Jacqui. As she said in one of her letters to Mrs. Plaister, she was always being amazed!

The homestead was furnished comfortably and in good taste. Nothing that made life easier and more enjoyable was left out. Even the kitchen was modern.

Gradually Jacqui met the staff, the five jackeroos, the six mechanics. They rarely came to the homestead, having their own kitchen and chef. Roars of laughter drifted from their single-storied building every night, and sometimes singing.

One day, surprisingly, Sally took her to see the abo village, half a mile away.

'Can you drive?' Sally asked, her voice dubious.

'Of course.'

'Good, then ask Uncle Alain if we can have one of the Rovers. We'll see the village and drive around.'

That started a new routine. Every day, either early in the morning or late afternoon, the children and Jacqui climbed into the spruce Land Rover and went for a drive, sometimes to the beautifully-planned abo village, with its neat houses and small gardens, its school and small church.

'Uncle Alain designed it all. He had it built,' Sally said, her voice proud.

Kangaroos were another source of fascination for Jacqui. She still could not see them as 'vermin', though Alain assured her that they were.

'A real nuisance,' he said. 'Out here we have to survive and can't afford to get sentimental over animals.'

Sometimes they drove to the creek. Here they would sit under one of the trees and watch the kangaroos as they came with their strangely fascinating jumps to the water.

'Uncle Alain's lucky,' Sally said one day. 'They've plenty of water here. In some places we have droughts for seven years.' She said it almost proudly.

'Seven years!' Jacqui whistled softly. 'Boy, that must be tough.'

'It certainly is. You just see the cattle dying and . . .'

'Sally!' Gaynor said quickly. He'd gone quite white.

'Sorry,' Sally said quickly. 'Look . . . Jacqui, did you know that when a baby kangaroo is born, it's only an inch long?'

'No ! Now that I can't believe!'

'It is. You ask Uncle Alain.'

I will, Jacqui thought, when I see him! Since her return to normal life she had very seldom seen him. Occasionally he came in for a meal, but his face was always thoughtful and he spoke little, then he would vanish back to his 'single-storied house', or go off in the plane or one of the Rovers.

'He's a hard worker, our Alain,' Cousin Adela said proudly one morning, surprising Jacqui, for the small energetic old woman rarely gave a word of praise. 'A good man,' Cousin Adela went on, then looked ashamed as if her words had shown a weakness on her part, so she added quickly: 'Eat up, children, I don't want to have you hanging around for ever.'

Now in the heat, brushing the flies away—would she ever get used to them crawling over her skin?—watching the kangaroos, Jacqui asked Sally: 'But how, if the baby kangaroo is only an inch long, does it live?'

56

Sally was always glad of the chance to show her knowledge and her superiority to the Pommie.

'Well, it's like this . . . the baby's born and crawls up his mummy's tummy to the pouch. Inside that there's a little teat and he clings to it and stays there until he's quite big.'

'You're kidding me,' Jacqui accused.

Sally roared with laughter. 'I am not! You ask Uncle Alain.'

'No, I believe you, Sally.'

The lanky girl looked startled. 'You do? Good-oh! D'you know what a mother kangaroo is called? You don't? Well, it's a doe and a male is a boomer, and a baby kangaroo is a joey. You don't know anything.'

'I'm not an Aussie. I bet you don't know . . .' Jacqui paused and tried to think of some English animal Sally could never have heard of. 'I bet you don't know what animal it is in the Loch Ness.'

'I do, too!' Sally yelled with delight. 'The Loch Ness monster!'

'I give up. You're too clever for me,' Jacqui confessed, laughing.

This was one of Sally's 'good days', days when she was friendly and joked, but there were many other days when she was sullen, cheeky and would vanish for hours at a time.

'Don't interfere,' Jacqui told herself silently. 'Remember what Alain said.'

Sometimes they had picnics. Then Gaynor

would collect driftwood for the fire and they would boil the 'billycan' and eat sandwiches cut by the aboriginal Sarah. Once there was a weird sound and Jacqui jumped. Sally looked scornful.

'That's only a dingo,' she said.

Jacqui enjoyed the lessons that came over the transceiver. It fascinated her and she always sat with the children as they worked. Sally usually asked Jacqui to answer some of the questions given and was delighted if Jacqui had to confess she didn't know.

It was as if Sally hated all adults—for, although she sometimes teased Jacqui and called her 'the Tall Teenager', Jacqui was still an adult in her eyes—and any victory she achieved over an adult delighted her. It was almost like a vendetta. Another strange thing was that the children rarely mentioned their parents. Surely that was unusual, Jacqui would think, and then reminded herself of Alain's 'lecture' and his advice to her to mind her own business! But Jacqui was growing fond of the children and their silence about their parents worried her, for it didn't seem natural.

Of course the transceiver featured in many of Jacqui's letters to Mrs. Plaister. It is absolutely fabulous, Jacqui wrote, our nearest neighbour is a hundred miles away. Yes, one hundred miles! But when we have a get-together on the transceiver, we all chat away as if we're in the same room.

Of course it was Sally who introduced Jacqui into the mysteries, who showed her which handle to turn when she wanted to talk, and which when she was listening. Most mornings they listened to the questions and answers given to the Flying Doctor, and Jacqui found herself looking forward to hearing Danny Mullins's voice, his jokes, quick laughter. He often sent her a message.

'And how is our new Pommie?' he would joke. 'Getting fond of the flies yet, my lovely lady?'

Everyone liked Danny. Except, Jacqui thought one day, Alain. Whenever Alain mentioned Danny's name, there was an almost imperceptible change in his voice, as if he disapproved. Yet what was there to disapprove of in the friendly and obviously respected Irish doctor? She was also fascinated by the medicine box and the way the different medicines each had a number.

'I think it's wonderful . . .' Jacqui said, and the two children were convulsed with laughter.

'Glad someone finds something to laugh at in life,' Cousin Adela said disapprovingly from the doorway. 'What's it this time?'

Jacqui looked up from the comfortable chair she was curled up in, her shoes on the ground. 'The children say I'm always saying how fascinating or wonderful Australia is.'

'Of course it is. A fine country. The finest in the world,' grunted Cousin Adela. 'I don't see anything funny in that.'

The Galah session came on and the small white-haired old woman left them, still mumbling her grumbles.

There was the usual gaggle of voices. Somehow the girl at the other end managed to sort them out and let them come in one at a time. Strange voices that after a few days became the voices of friends, always asking after Jacqui, saying they were sorry she'd been ill to start with—the 'doc' had told them, it seemed. The voices asked her questions about how she liked Australia and all seemed delighted to hear she liked it very much indeed.

'But I can't get used to the flies,' Jacqui would say.

'You will,' they promised her. 'You've got no choice.'

Sometimes they exchanged recipes or talked of a letter received from a son or daughter seeking fame in distant London or New York.

Often Jacqui and Gaynor would sit at the piano and play duets while Sally went off for a ride. Sometimes Jacqui would try to compose music while Gaynor made up the words. Actually Jacqui enjoyed these musical sessions the most in her new way of living, for Gaynor seemed to really relax and treat her as a friend.

One morning the three of them were on the verandah, discussing some difficult work set during the lesson session. For once, Jacqui knew more than Sally and was trying to give Sally the knowledge diplomatically, without sounding superior. There was a sound of a plane overhead and Jacqui looked out through the screen.

'That's Andrea,' said Sally. 'She's our nearest neighbour. She's always flying over, but she's been away, that's why you haven't met her.'

'Usually she's always here,' said Gaynor. 'She's in love with . . . ouch!' he cried out in pain.

Jacqui looked round. Sally was looking innocent and Gaynor was rubbing his ankle and scowling at his sister.

Turning away to watch the plane circle and start to come down on the strip, Jacqui found herself wondering what it was Gaynor had been about to say when Sally kicked him.

'She's in love with . . .' Gaynor had said. Had he been going to add 'Alain'?

'Now she'll stay for lunch and Uncle Alain will come and . . .' Sally grumbled.

'Don't you like her?'

Sally looked at Jacqui. 'She's all right, but she's . . . she's square!'

Later, when Alain drove his visitor over to the homestead to meet Jacqui, Jacqui wondered what on earth Sally could have meant. As the tall, slender, truly beautiful girl came to meet her, hand outstretched in a

61

friendly way, Jacqui thought she had never met anyone so nice.

'Jacqui, welcome to the Outback, though I'm afraid I'm a bit late. Danny tells me you were ill at first. Everything all right now?' Andrea Rank asked, sinking with incredible gracefulness into the chair by Jacqui's side while Alain hurried off to get them long cool drinks.

'I'm fine, thanks,' Jacqui replied.

She found it hard not to stare at Andrea. She had never seen anyone so beautiful before, with that cloud of jet black hair hanging down her back, the dark lovely eyes, the friendly smile.

'I'm Alain's nearest neighbour,' Andrea explained. 'Both my parents are dead and I manage my own station with Alain's advice.' She smiled at him. 'I honestly don't know how I'd have managed without you, Alain.'

He laughed. 'I'm sure you would have, Andrea. You're a very efficient woman.'

Andrea pretended to pout as she looked at Jacqui. 'I ask you! The gallant Australian. What woman wants to be called *efficient?* Nearly as bad as being told you have a kind face!'

'Well, you have a kind face,' Alain said, and ducked as Andrea threw a cushion at him.

Andrea, as well as being beautiful and friendly, was also very witty, Jacqui found, as they had lunch. Grumbling as usual, Cousin

Adela accepted Andrea's compliments on the delicious food. Alain and Andrea entered into a lively but amicable argument while the children and Jacqui ate silently.

Jacqui wasn't sure why, but suddenly she felt young and gauche. Maybe it was the way Alain spoke to her, kindly, almost condescendingly. He seemed to be coupling her with the children. Maybe he was, because he had made it plain he found her very young, much too young to travel right across the world alone!

After lunch, the children vanished and Jacqui found herself alone with Andrea. They went into the garden behind the homestead and heard the children laughing in the swimming pool. There was a canopy on poles to make a shady place for the swing chair and Andrea suggested they sat there.

'How are you settling down?' she asked anxiously. 'I know England well and you must find it very different here.'

'I find it both fascinating and exciting. I didn't realise people were so wealthy and lived such luxurious lives.'

Andrea laughed. 'Don't get misled, Jacqui. Kiah isn't typical of all Australia. This was always a wealthy station, but Alain's skill and industry has made it one of the wealthiest in the state.' She spoke proudly. 'He's a fine man, Jacqui, a hard worker and something of a genius. He's also an idealist and does a

63

tremendous amount of good. Have you seen the abo village? Isn't it fine?'

'Yes. Then . . . then all farmers aren't so successful?'

Andrea laughed. 'Goodness, no! Some time I must arrange a tour for you, Jacqui. I'd hate you to leave Australia and think everyone's as wealthy as this. Some of my farming friends are battling. Alain is lucky in that he has an unlimited supply of water. Few stations have that. Even I haven't. Drought is my biggest foe. Of course when the wet comes . . . By the way, is Cousin Adela very difficult?'

Jacqui hesitated. 'Not exactly difficult, but . . . well, she thinks I'm too young . . . and, it wasn't very good my being ill when I got here.'

Andrea was laughing. 'No, you certainly got off on the wrong foot, Jacqui. She loathes illness. She's had too much of it.'

'She's been ill?'

'No. I doubt if she's had a day's illness in her sixty-two years. No, she was always nursing members of the family. First her grandfather, then her parents, then Alain's mother after his father's death . . .'

'I didn't know that,' said Jacqui, remembering Alain's remarks about Cousin Adela's bitterness and resentment.

'She doesn't talk about it, but it's common knowledge that when she was a girl, she lost the man she was going to marry because her parents wouldn't let her go. They said they needed her. Poor Adela! She's really very kind, but . . . And the children?'

Again Jacqui hesitated. 'We get on all right, but . . .'

'But . . .' Andrea echoed. She lifted her soft black hair with one hand and let it drop slowly. '*But*. Poor little brats!'

'Poor little brats?'

Andrea nodded. 'Well, can you blame them for being difficult when they were treated as they were?'

'I don't know how they were treated.'

'Didn't Alain tell you? Well, Sally and Gaynor and their parents were all set for a trip to New Zealand when his father had to go to London on business. That upset the children, because this holiday had been promised for a long time and they adore their father . . . and then their mother brought them here. Alain was away, and she just left them. They knew nothing about it. They went to bed one night and in the morning their mother was gone. She'd arranged for a plane to fetch her, but she hadn't even told the kids.'

'Oh, how awful! She just vanished?'

'Exactly. About the meanest thing a mother could do. But Cecile is like that. Never thinks of anyone else.'

'It explains a lot . . .' Jacqui said thoughtfully 'An awful lot.'

'Cousin Adela was also very upset,' Andrea continued. 'You see, she had no idea they were coming. Cecile and the children flew in without warning. The plane went off again. Next morning when Cousin Adela got up, Cecile had gone. The plane had come in to pick her up. I imagine Adela heard the plane but thought it was one of the planes used on the station.

Anyhow, you can imagine the shock the children had when they found their mother had gone.'

'I most certainly can,' Jacqui said slowly. 'How could anyone do such a cruel thing?'

Andrea shrugged. 'If you knew Cecile you'd understand. She's a superb egoist. Maybe it's not her fault. Her parents—and Alain's—were cold, unemotional folk who saw it as a weakness to express love in any form. Alain, as a result, retreated behind a barrier of self-containment. Cecile became possessive and jealous. Cecile loves her husband—worships him. My guess is that she followed him to England because she didn't know why he'd gone there. But it still isn't fair to the children. Nor has she written to them.'

'How hurt they must be. That explains why they hardly ever mention her name,' Jacqui said thoughtfully. 'How can any woman . . .'

Andrea stood up. 'I must go and talk business with Alain. I'll be flying home later, so I won't see you again this time, Jacqui, but I won't forget the tour I want to arrange. While you're up here, I'd like you to see more of the

Outback and how we live!' She smiled. 'I'm so glad Alain got a nice person like you for the children. I felt so sorry for them, dumped here like unwanted rubbish.'

The words remained in Jacqui's mind. Was that how Sally and Gaynor felt? she wondered. That they were, to their mother, 'unwanted rubbish'?

*   *   *

That evening Alain came to the homestead to eat; afterwards, he and Jacqui sat on the screened verandah. The sky sparkled with stars and there was a strangely eerie stillness.

When Jacqui remarked on this, Alain stretched out his legs and laughed. 'Wait until the men start singing. They're busy eating right now.'

'I haven't seen Ruggles lately,' Jacqui began.

Alain laughed again. 'You will! He's around. I gave him a brief holiday. I usually do while I'm here and don't need him. By the way, how did you get on with Andrea? She liked you. She approved of my choice of governess.' He smiled. 'She thought it was a good thing you were so young as it bridged the gulf between adults and Sally.'

As Jacqui poured out two fresh cups of coffee, she was thinking fast. Just what had Andrea told him? She wondered. That she knew about the way the children's mother had behaved? Or would Alain, if she mentioned this, accuse her of 'interfering' and of being 'inquisitive'? He had warned her before, but really this time she had asked *no* questions. Andrea had volunteered the information, as if she thought Jacqui should know. Which she should, Jacqui thought, for it helped her understand and condone Sally's strange behaviour, poor darling.

Jacqui put down her cup and looked at the silent man. 'I thought she was the most beautiful woman I've ever seen,' she said truthfully, 'and one of the nicest.'

Alain stirred his coffee and nodded. He seemed pleased.

'You're so right, Jacqui, my word you are! Andrea *is* one of the most beautiful women I know, and as you say, one of the nicest. I've never heard her say a malicious word, or be catty or unkind.'

'I just can't understand why . . .' Jacqui began, and then stopped speaking, arrested by the amused look in his eyes. She felt the slow hot flush cover her cheeks. 'I know,' she said miserably. 'You'll say I'm at it again, but I still can't understand why anyone so nice and so lovely is still single.'

Alain was smiling. 'Honestly, Jacqui, I sometimes wonder under what sort of conditions you were reared! Were you brought up to believe that the ultimate heaven of every

68

woman is to be a wife?'

Her cheeks burned still more. 'Well, isn't it?'

His smile vanished. 'Could be you're right, and I'm wrong,' he said gravely. 'But I can't see that this can apply to *every* woman, Jacqui. I meet a lot of brilliant, intellectual career women who are not married yet seem completely happy.'

'The thing is when you get old . . .' Jacqui began, twisting her fingers together unhappily.

He was smiling again. 'My dear Jacqui, are you suggesting most women marry as an insurance against a lonely old age?'

'Of course not, but . . . well, I'm thinking of my Aunt Elspeth. I mean, she had absolutely no one, except me. I've known lots of old people—you get to know them in a village— men and women who have been awfully lonely in their old age. I'd hate to go through life living alone. I want a husband and lots of children and grandchildren . . .'

Alain was laughing and he held up his hand. 'And great-grandchildren and so on, ad infinitum. How ghastly it sounds, and all to avoid loneliness!'

Her cheeks burned again. 'No, that makes it sound so selfish. I want a family that I can love and look after, people to whom I mean something important. I'm tired of belonging to nobody, for Aunt Elspeth didn't really want me, she just put up with me because it was her duty.'

'All right, let's start again in the first square. You want to marry because you've never had a family. Right? Well, how can you guarantee that if you marry, your husband's family will open its arms for you?'

'We'll make our own family.'

'All right, you'll make your own family. How can you be sure your children will love you? Look how difficult young Sally is . . .'

'How can you blame her,' Jacqui's indignation overcame her discretion, 'after the terrible way her mother treated her?' Her hand flew to her mouth in dismay. Her eyes were the wide frightened eyes of a child as she stared at Alain. 'I didn't ask questions,' she added lamely.

His smile was a relief. 'My word, Jacqui, be your age! I'm not going to bite your head off. I imagine Andrea told you?'

'Yes. She . . . she was so sorry for them.'

'I know. She told me in no uncertain terms. Mind if I smoke? Thanks. The whole point is,' he went on as he slowly packed his pipe, 'that Andrea doesn't realise how Cecile and I view life. Perhaps we are selfish, but it's the way we've been brought up. We have what you might call 'single eyes'. There's one thing we want and we go after it. My 'single eye' has been sublimated in my work. I'm determined that it shall be perfect, or as near perfect as man can make it. That's why I'm a happy man,

70

Jacqui. I have an aim, to make a success of farming, to test and make use of every modern invention that can improve farming. My eyes are centred on that aim and nothing else in life really counts. Are you shocked?'

She was. 'You mean, no person counts?' Then *he* wasn't in love with Andrea, she was thinking.

He laughed. 'Not at the moment. My work comes first, second and last. Maybe one day . . .' He shrugged his massive shoulders. 'Who knows?'

'And . . . and your sister's 'single eye'?'

He sighed and his smile vanished. 'Is, I'm afraid, her husband. She worships the ground he walks on and he can twist her round his little finger. Unfortunately he knows this and does it, so he causes her much unnecessary sorrow and anxiety. She's possessive and jealous and he seems to delight in arousing these emotions.'

'But how could she just dump the children?'

He shrugged again. 'She took the easiest way out. Cecile always did. She can't bear an emotional scene and would do anything to avoid one. The kids adore their father and had been counting on this trip to New Zealand. I blame *him* for not explaining to them why they couldn't go. Instead he just walked out on them. Cecile, I imagine, thought of me at once as someone she could leave the kids with, so dumped them here, as you so aptly put it, and then followed Henry. Had she told the children she was going to their father, they'd have created scenes. Gaynor becomes quite ill when he's emotionally upset, and Sally has terrible tantrums. That's why, I imagine, Cecile just left them here.'

'I think it was a terrible thing to do.'

'So do I, but don't we all do terrible things at some time or another? It's none of our business, but I expect Cecile was nearly ill with fear of losing Henry and she could only think of that. She knew the kids would be all right with me.'

'But are they?' Jacqui answered. 'Gaynor retreats into himself. It's a real battle to get him to relax and enjoy anything. Sally's moods are surely a sign that she resents the treatment she was given. After all, she's not a child. She's thirteen, and . . . and lots of girls marry in their teens these days, so she's definitely old enough to be told the truth . . . She stopped, aware that Alain was smiling at her—not nastily; indeed it was a kind smile, but touched with condescension.

'Jacqui, I just hope you retain your ideals and zeal to help others. It's rather wonderful in this day and age, but don't try to reform the world. You won't succeed and will only make enemies or hurt people. You can help the children best by doing what you are— accepting them, showing them you enjoy being with them, giving them a feeling, however

72

temporary, of security. In time we shall hear from Cecile and everything will work itself out. Everything does, you know. It's an old cliché, but time is a great healer. I should know.'

'You heart was broken?' In her surprise, Jacqui used words she would not normally have done.

Alain's laughter was her answer. He shook his head as he laughed.

'My poor Jacqui, you've got love on the brain! Yes, my heart was broken, but not by a woman. It's a long story. Interested? Yes, I can see you are. Your eyes are like stars, your ears are pointed as you lean forward eagerly! Tell me, Jacqui, just why are you so interested in other people?'

Again she felt that slow heat in her cheeks. 'I don't know. I've always been interested in people. Maybe living in a village . . .'

He relit his pipe, cupping the flame from the silver lighter in his hand. 'Well, it's nice to meet someone these days who does care about people. I'm only afraid it may land you in trouble one day. No one so naive and innocent as you ought to be let loose in the world alone. I think it's a great pity you haven't parents and the security of a home.'

'I can look after myself,' Jacqui began indignantly.

'I sincerely hope so, but when I look at you, Jacqui, my sympathy grows for fathers of beautiful young girls. If you were my daughter,

73

I'd lock you up in a tower to keep you safe.'

Her indignation was growing. 'Alain, that's absolutely absurd! It's like feeding your children on sterilised food lest they eat a germ and then the first time they eat ordinary food they're ill. Facing up to tricky situations is part of growing mature. I promise you I'm capable of taking care of myself. I'm nearly nineteen and I haven't been hurt yet.'

'Because you lived in a small village under the watchful eye of your aunt and the lady who keeps 'umbrellas'. Now you're out in the world, and you're as vulnerable as a sitting duck.'

'Well, I've been called some names, but this is the first time I was called a sitting duck,' Jacqui said with a laugh.

'D'you know one of the nicest things about you, Jacqui?' Alain asked as he tapped out his pipe, then began to pack it again. 'One can tease you to the point of fury, but you overcome it every time. You bite, but you control your temper. A worthy talent!' He smiled. 'Well, ready for the long saga of how Alain Hollington's heart was broken?'

Jacqui kicked off her shoes, tucked her legs under her, resting her elbow on the arm of the chair, her chin on her hand. Had she had any idea of how lovely she looked, with her pointed face and soft curly hair, her interested eyes, she'd have been both surprised and embarrassed.

'Please, my ears are cocked in readiness!'

He laughed. 'Well, it all began some twenty years ago. I was just a kid, about ten. Gaynor's age. My parents were rather . . . you'd call them cold, I'd call them self-contained and self-disciplined. Tears or groans were a sign of weakness. We had a neighbour, an old tramp, hobo . . . whatever you like to call him. A remittance man from England. He'd been a naughty lad in his youth and his family, high up in the aristocracy, paid him an allowance to keep out of the country. He ended up here in a small hut. He was supposed to be going round the bend.'

Alain laughed. 'I guess kids of ten can be pretty romantic if they'll admit it. I called him the Duke of Araby. Don't ask me where I got the name. Maybe I invented it. He was a bent old man with grizzled grey hair, always too long. How he talked! I could sit for hours and listen to him. He was a specialist in history, which fascinated me. He made things that happened hundreds of years ago come to life. When I got sent to boarding school I missed him. One holiday I came home and he was gone.'

His face changed, became grave. 'I was upset. I tried to hide it. In the end, my mother lost patience and told me old Parkins was a murderer and had been hanged. I couldn't believe it—that he was a murderer. I remembered the way he handled sick animals,

75

the tenderness, the love, he showed. He had two cats as well as a very old sheepdog. I reckon they were fed better than he ever was. I tried to find out what he'd done, but everyone clamped down. I was seventeen before I broke through the wall erected round his memory. I was like a maniac as I studied every note, every word of any witness's evidence. I was certain he was innocent. In the end, there was an enquiry and he was exonerated. A mistake had been made, only it happened to be six years too late, for he was dead. Somehow or other his counsel had overlooked vital evidence. It shook me . . .'

He paused, smiled at Jacqui. 'It doesn't sound like me, does it? My family were livid. They said I was wasting my time, that it couldn't do the old man any good. They couldn't see it was his *name* I was saving. I wanted his family, who despised him, to know the truth. It was then I knew what I was going to do with my life.'

Jacqui waited, her eyes large and wondering.

'Well, I decided to be a lawyer. One day I would be a counsel and I'd work for all the folk who couldn't afford to pay for a lawyer.' Alain gave an odd laugh. 'You see, we've been rich for a long time. I could afford to work for very little or even nothing. I went to university to study law. I think those were the happiest years of my life. I was achieving an ambition.

76

I was going to be the greatest lawyer ever.' He laughed, relaxing and stretching his long legs. 'Then . . .'

'Then?'

He lost his smile. 'Fate took a hand. My father and my two brothers were all killed in the same airplane crash. My mother sent for me as she was alone with Cecile. My mother had always been something of an invalid and knew nothing about the station. So I gave up law and became a farmer.'

He smiled at Jacqui. 'The story of my broken heart. Yes, it did hurt, at first. I still read books on law and am fascinated by it. But this was my job and I've done it well. Now I love it.' He stood up, smiling down at her.

'I hope you're happy now you know what makes me tick.'

She stood up, smiling up at him. 'Thanks for telling me. I think it was pretty wonderful of you.'

He shrugged. 'What choice had I? Now, it would have been wonderful had I had a brother who loathed farming and I stood in for him against my own wishes. Come outside and look at the night. The moon's coming up.'

Jacqui hastily put on her sandals and followed him through the door. Here the mosquitoes and moths were banging themselves against the wire screens, trying to get through to the tempting lights.

Alain helped her down the steps, his hand

77

casually on her bare arm. The night was very still. Even the men in the staff quarters were quiet. In the distance a dingo howled. The moon was round and orange in the black sky, the stars sparkling.

'I'm so glad I took Mrs. Plaister's advice,' Jacqui said suddenly, 'and came out here. I'd hate to have missed Australia. It's so beautiful, so wonderfully exciting.' She turned eagerly to him. 'There's so much to be done out here, so much to learn, so much to explore. She was right. I want to see the world, then I'll settle down in a small suburban house with a family of noisy brats and I'll be able to look back and remember. She says memories are something we need.'

'She is, I take it, a great romanticist and believes in happiness ever after, once the wedding bells have rung.'

Jacqui turned to try to see the expression on his face. 'And you don't?'

'Frankly, no.'

'But. . .'

He laughed. 'Please, Jacqui, don't look so distressed for me. I'm a cynic. So many of my friends have broken marriages or live in unhappy conditions. Maybe one day I will fall in love and think it's worth the gamble, for gamble it is. When you come to think of it, before you take a partner into a firm, you make copious enquiries, demand references, etc., etc., but when you marry . . . well, I've

78

known people marry after knowing one another for a few weeks and that's all. When I marry, I'm going to be very sure.'

'Perhaps that's how Andrea feels.'

He turned his hand on her arm as they walked back to the steps. 'Poor Andrea suffers from a terrible complication. She happens to be a very wealthy woman. She inherited money from her grandparents as well as her parents. Her station is very well run. She's efficient and conscientious. A great many men have proposed to her, but she comes up against that obstacle that so often hackles the wealthy woman: "Does he love me, or my money?" You see, she's got to be very sure, too.'

Jacqui stared up at him. 'But if a very wealthy man proposed . . .'

She saw he was smiling. 'Well, Jacqui, that might be the solution, but if she had any sense, she'll put her solicitors to work and make sure the very wealthy man isn't bordering on the slopes of bankruptcy.'

'How awful! One thing . . .' Jacqui smiled as they left the mosquito-ridden air and the door closed behind them, 'I need never worry about that, because I've got nothing.'

He hesitated for a moment, staring down at her. 'You may not have any money, Jacqui, but you have a great deal to offer any man.' He gave her no time to answer. 'Good night, Jacqui,' he said, and turned away, going out of doors and back to his small house.

Jacqui went to her room. It was hot, but the lofty room with the big screened windows was inviting. She wondered who had chosen the azure blue curtains that matched the carpet, or the delightful suite of satinwood. A lovely, inviting room. She had a refreshing shower and went to bed.

But she didn't feel sleepy. So she took out her writing pad. She was always writing to Mrs. Plaister these days.

'I think Alain likes to pretend he's tough and a cynic, but underneath that self-possessed exterior, I think he's as romantic as anyone. My guess is that he's in love with Andrea and she with him but that both are scared of marriage. It seems such a shame, because they're both such nice people. I am really loving life here, but I do wish I could find a way to make the children happy. I feel so sorry for them. Surely their mother could write, or even send a postcard,' she wrote, yawned, put away her writing case and fell asleep.

The next day Danny Mullins came. He also brought a sack of mail. There were two letters for Jacqui, one from Mrs. Plaister and the other from Kay Dunn. The children too had mail. Each had a card. One was of Tower Bridge; the second was of the Houses of Parliament. No real message on either card, just 'Love from us both, Mummy'.

Sally tore her postcard up into tiny pieces, tearing each piece apart with an alarming viciousness, her mouth a thin line, her eyes smouldering. Jacqui pretended to be absorbed in the book she was reading, but she also saw the way Gaynor stared at the postcard, put it on the table and walked out of the room. Did Alain's sister really think a postcard of London was enough? Or was that all she had time for?

Luckily Dr. Mullins helped the situation, as he stayed to lunch, telling jokes, making even the children's dour faces crease into lines of laughter.

Afterwards he sat with Jacqui and the children as they drank coffee on the verandah. He asked a few medical-inspired questions, felt her pulse, looked pleased.

'You've adapted yourself well. That attack was sheer bad luck. Could have happened to anyone at any time,' he said.

Overhead a plane roared. A quick smile crossed Gaynor's face, but then he looked at his sister and pretended to be absorbed in the drawing game he was doing, making circles and triangles into patterns.

Danny Mullins looked up. 'Sounds like Andrea's plane. Expecting her?'

'I wasn't. She was here yesterday. I know she and Alain were talking business.'

'Were they?' said Danny, his thin humorous face grave. 'I believe he advises her. You liked her?'

'Oh, very much indeed,' Jacqui smiled at

him. 'Don't you think she's really beautiful? That lovely jet black hair, those eyes, that marvellous skin . . .'

'I rather go for brown hair with a curly fringe,' he told her, his eyes twinkling.

'Then your taste isn't as good as Alain's.'

'He thinks she's beautiful.'

Jacqui nodded. 'Yes, he agreed with me. That she was beautiful and very nice. He said she was brilliantly intellectual, conscientious and . . .'

'Perfect,' Danny supplied the word with a wry smile. 'I'm afraid I don't make the grade.'

Jacqui was on her feet as the children opened the screened door. The car drew up and Ruggles got out to open the door for Andrea, who was sitting alone at the back of the car.

'Neither do I,' Jacqui was saying. 'I'm too young, I'm afraid.'

But Danny wasn't listening. He was staring at the tall slim girl with the beautiful black hair now twisted round her head, the dark eyes, her slender body in a beautifully-cut cream tussore suit.

She held out her hands, her face bright with pleasure. 'Why, Danny Mullins! How lovely to see you. I didn't realise this was your day to come here.'

Cousin Adela was suddenly there, at Jacqui's elbow, her face disapproving. 'It was
82

on the air this morning,' she said dourly.

Andrea laughed. 'I'm afraid I overslept. I had a pretty late night, so I was tired.'

'You'll have eaten?' Cousin Adela said.

Andrea gave Jacqui a rueful look and then smiled. 'I'm not hungry. I'd love a cup of coffee and maybe a cheese sandwich if that's not too much trouble.'

'Let me get it,' Jacqui began.

The short wiry woman with the snow-white hair glared at her.

'Haven't I told you to keep out of my kitchen?'

'I thought perhaps I could help.'

'I need no help, never have done and never will,' Cousin Adela grumbled as she went off.

Andrea tossed her long white gloves on the table and sat down, smiling at them all. 'You just can't win, Jacqui. I gave up trying long ago.' She looked at the children. 'Ever been to the Picnic Races?'

Sally's sullen face began to relax. 'No. I've always wanted to go, but. . . I'd love to go, wouldn't you Gaynor? Why?'

'I was thinking it would be nice if we could all go, show Jacqui something of the neighbours. You'll be going, Danny?'

'Of course. Wouldn't miss it for anything.' He smiled at Jacqui. 'It's really quite something, Jacqui. Got its own character. Hot, my word, I'll say! But worth it. Then they have a dance in the evening . . .'

'I can't see Alain staying for that,' Andrea laughed. 'Can you?'

'Will Uncle Alain come?' Sally asked.

'I hope so. I'll ask him.'

'Then he will come,' said Gaynor.

There was an awkward little silence which they broke by all speaking at once. This made the silence before even more noticeable.

'Is it real racing?'

'Noisy, but great fun, Jacqui.'

'Your uncle may be too busy.'

'The dance wouldn't be much fun.'

Then they all looked at one another and there was a sort of uneasy laugh. Fortunately Sarah came out carrying a tray and the awkward moment was passed.

Later Andrea described her plan. 'I want you to meet people, Jacqui. I'm going to ask Alain to lend us Ruggles so that he can drive you and the children. . .' She paused to smile at the silent Sally and Gaynor. 'I hope you'll come. Well, we'll plan where we're going and Ruggles can drive you and I'll meet you there. Save me coming here first. Lots of people want to meet you, Jacqui. You do play tennis?'

'She plays tennis, water-skis, sails a boat, milks a cow, nurses a pig and plays the piano,' Sally chanted, her face alight for a brief moment, giving them all a glimpse of the sort of girl she normally was, when not in one of her moods. 'She speaks four or five languages, does shorthand and typing. But she didn't

84

know that a kangaroo's baby is only an inch long and I don't think she believes me now.'

'I do, too, Sally,' Jacqui said between laughter which they all shared. 'It sounds a marvellous idea, Andrea, and awfully good of you.'

Andrea smiled, her lovely face even more beautiful. 'My pleasure, Jacqui. I think we'll all enjoy it. Does us good to break away for a change. This sort of life can become a prison if you don't watch out.' She jumped up. 'I'll go and see Alain now. I did speak to Ruggles and he was quite keen. He likes getting around a bit. See you later!' She waved her hand and went outside.

There was a silence when she had gone. Jacqui looked at Sally.

'You two would come, wouldn't you?' she asked earnestly. 'I'm shy and . . . it would help me.'

Gaynor leaned against her shoulder showing her the design he had drawn. 'Look at this pattern, Jacqui. What d'you see?' he asked, and added, 'Of course we'll come.' He glared across the room at Sally. 'Won't we?'

It was unusual for Gaynor to stand up to his big sister and Jacqui was surprised; even more surprised at Sally's sweet smile as she replied, 'Of course we will if Jacqui needs us.'

Jacqui blinked fast, but Danny had seen the brief glimpse of tears in her eyes. He waited for Sally to go off to look at the horses and

85

Gaynor to go to play the piano, his fingers soft and surprisingly articulate as he touched the keys. Then Danny leaned forward and looked gravely at Jacqui.

'I told you they'd like you,' he said softly. 'Who could help it?'

CHAPTER FOUR

Jacqui and the children went along to the airstrip to say goodbye to Andrea. She was looking as beautiful as usual. Jacqui, in her thin green frock, smiled.

'I wish you didn't make me feel such a child,' she said impulsively.

Andrea laughed. 'My dear Jacqui, I wish the same in reverse. Looking at you, I feel about a hundred!'

She was gone with a wave of her hand. Watching the casually efficient way Andrea managed the plane, Jacqui sighed. How wonderful to be both beautiful and clever.

'She's nice,' Gaynor said unexpectedly.

Jacqui, walking with the two children back towards the homestead, smiled. 'Very nice indeed.'

'She's all right,' Sally said grudgingly. 'She's not bad.'

'I'm looking forward to the trips, Sally, but I'm a bit scared. I haven't played much tennis for a year and . . .' she gave a little rueful smile, 'I was wondering if we could practise?'

Sally's smile was condescending. 'Sure.'

Gaynor chimed in, 'I warn you she's good, Jacqui.'

Sally was beaming now. She blossomed when praised, Jacqui noted silently. Maybe that was what Sally needed—more appreciation, more boosting of her ego.

'Maybe Jacqui's good,' Sally added.

Jacqui made a silent resolution to play cleverly but to let Sally win.

'We'll have to play early in the morning or after tea. It soon gets dark, but in the heat . . .' Sally was saying.

Four motor-bikes came roaring by them, heading for the garage.

'Where do they go?' Jacqui asked. 'I'm always seeing them and keep forgetting to ask you.'

Sally sighed. 'Honestly, Jacqui, you know nothing. They've been rounding up the cattle.'

'I thought they did that on horses.'

Sally sighed again. 'So they do—near home, but lots of cattle are nearly a hundred miles away so they have to use motor-bikes.'

'Well, do they round up sheep on motor-bikes too? I mean, what's happened to the old sheepdog?'

'Oh, Jacqui, you're always asking questions!' Sally scolded.

'I don't know about sheep. We used to keep

87

cattle.'

'Haven't you got a farm . . . I mean, station, now?' Jacqui asked without thinking.

Both the children looked at her and she saw dismay on their faces, and silently cursed herself for asking such a leading question. Anything to do with their parents or their home life seemed to be taboo. In an effort to save the situation she plunged into a different subject.

'You can't think how I envy you both, having one another.'

Some of Sally's dismay vanished into surprise. 'You haven't *any* brothers or sisters?'

They'd reached the homestead by now and sat on the verandah, comparatively safe from the ravages of the flies. Jacqui could hear Cousin Adela's grumbling voice in the kitchen as she cooked the evening meal.

Jacqui kicked off her shoes and curled up on the couch. She saw she'd caught the children's attention. 'Frankly, I've got no one. No one at all.'

'No one?' Gaynor repeated slowly.

'No, no one. I was about six years old when both my parents died . . .' Jacqui said the word hastily, 'and I went to an orphanage. In the holidays I stayed with my Aunt Elspeth usually.'

'What was she like?'

Jacqui plumped up the cushions and piled them behind her back. 'What was she like,

88

Sally? Well, she was tall and thin and had white hair. She was kind, but she was . . . well, d'you know what a perfectionist is?'

Sally nodded. 'Uncle Alain.'

Jacqui laughed. 'Oh, he's not as bad as Aunt Elspeth. I was almost afraid to move in her cottage in case I disturbed anything or got dirty. She taught music and did dressmaking and . . .'

'You were . . . you weren't unhappy?'

'Unhappy, Sally? I'm not sure that in those days I knew what it meant to be happy. At school I was always in trouble for fighting.' She began to laugh.

'You—fighting?' Gaynor looked disbelieving.

'Oh yes. You see, I was skinny and the other girls bullied me, but I wouldn't put up with it. I fought back. Unfortunately the nuns believed in 'turning the other cheek', so I was always in trouble. Then as I grew up, I found that I pleased my Aunt Elspeth if I got good reports, so I worked hard.'

'Why did you want to please her?'

'Why, Sally? Well, because I felt guilty. I wonder if you know what I mean? Someone is kind to you and . . . and you still can't love them. She was kind to me, she must have hated me being about, but she never said so. She was old, much older than my father, and I was young and noisy. Luckily there was a farm near us and a very nice farmer's wife.'

'Is that where you learned how to milk

a cow?'

'And nurse a pig?'

Jacqui laughed. 'Exactly. I loved farming. I always said that one day I'd marry a farmer, but . . . well, farmers in England are very different from farmers out here. Alain is more like a business executive than a farmer.'

'He's a very good farmer!'

Jacqui pretended to cower. 'All right, all right, I'm not running down your uncle, Sally. I know he's a good farmer. I just said that Aussie farmers are different from English ones.'

'Where did you learn to water-ski?' Gaynor asked.

'Oh, that was on one of the holidays. A school friend asked me home. She'd been adopted and left the orphanage, but she never forgot us—her friends, I mean. She and her new parents gave me a super time, Gaynor. We went on the Broads. That's in Norfolk and all water, lakes and river and estuaries. They had a ferry we lived on, and a small sailing boat and a motor boat. It was terrific!'

'We do a lot of water-skiing here, you know.' As usual Sally leapt to the defence of her country. 'Especially on the Gold Coast.'

'Gold Coast?'

'Oh, Jacqui, really! Haven't you ever heard of the Gold Coast? That's in Queensland with absolutely gorgeous beaches, and you can surf there, too.'

'It sounds terrific. Maybe one day I'll see it. Anyhow I had a wonderful holiday.'

'You must have hated going back to the orphanage,' Sally said unexpectedly.

Jacqui nodded. 'I did. I wished someone would adopt me, because I could see how happy Patricia was. It's a terrible feeling when you've got no parents—you feel unwanted . . .' She stopped abruptly, realising she was on dangerous ground. But even as she stopped, the door opened and Alain stood there.

He was looking at her oddly and she wondered how much he had heard. It made her feel ill at ease, for she hadn't meant to sound interfering or as if she was trying to get the kids to talk.

'Gaynor, run and get us two cold mints, will you? Sally, Roger was telling me that Sunrise hasn't been too fit. What d'you think? Like me to ask the vet to look in?'

Sally jumped up. 'I'll go and have a look, Uncle. I thought he looked better this morning.'

'Well, let me know, Sally, and I'll get on the transceiver.' He waited until she had gone and then sat down opposite Jacqui.

'Know something, Jacqui?' he began, taking out his pipe, tapping it on the ash tray. 'I never realised you'd had such an unhappy childhood. You're such a well- balanced, sensible, happy person.'

Jacqui straightened her skirt, sat upright,

91

thrusting her feet into her sandals. 'I didn't say I was unhappy, Alain, but I certainly wasn't happy. The nuns were kind, but they had to be impersonal. It's an awful feeling when you belong to no one, when no one loves you.'

'You had your aunt.'

'She didn't *love* me. She was kind, but I always had a feeling that she was doing her duty nobly. It's hard, you know, as a child, to know you're not important to anyone. It gave me an awful feeling of . . . perhaps the word is insecurity.'

'You show no sign of it now.' He was slowly packing his pipe, pulling out the long brown strands of tobacco.

Jacqui laughed. 'I was lucky. I made two wonderful friends, the farmer's wife who was a honey, and Mrs. Plaister. They made me feel loved and wanted.'

'You're always stressing love. D'you think it's so important to be loved?'

She looked up at him, brushing her hair back, but he wasn't laughing at her. He looked serious, almost as if he really wanted her opinion.

'I think that you just die if you're not loved,' she said simply. 'There's no reason left why you should live. Maybe your body goes on functioning, but inside you, you shrivel up and die.'

Gaynor returned at that moment, carefully carrying the tray, his tongue protruding through his lips a little, as it always did when he was tense. He sighed with relief as he put it on the table.

'Sally's having a look at the horses, Gaynor. Why not join her?'

Gaynor looked at his uncle and turned away, to go out through the door. Impulsively Jacqui turned to the man opposite who was handing her an ice cold glass.

'There, that's what I mean. I know you didn't intend to be unkind, but . . .'

She put down the glass and twisted her hands together.

'How can I explain? It happened to me so often. I would rush home, bursting with excitement to tell Aunt Elspeth about a baby lamb, or that a hen had laid an enormous egg, or something or other that seemed to me most terribly thrilling and she would look up and say quietly: "Go and wash your hands, Jacqueline, and lay the table for me". She never ever listened to me. It's terrible when you're young and no one listens. All the wonderful things that are happening to the world around you are bottled up inside you, wasted because you can't share them with anyone. Same with the children. You hardly ever talk to them. I know you don't mean it unkindly. I know you're most frightfully busy, but. . . but is money all that important? I mean, they are your niece and nephew and they are both terribly unhappy and worried about their parents . . .'

93

She paused and turned red.

'I'm sorry, Alain, I'm interfering again. I didn't mean . . .'

He leaned forward and lightly touched her hand. 'You were not interfering, Jacqui, but I hadn't thought of it like that. Frankly, I thought they'd rather I kept out of their way. I hardly know them, and . . .' He smiled. 'I'll be honest, I wanted to talk to you—alone.'

She was worried. Had she gone too far? Was he about to read her a lecture on not being a 'do-gooder'?

'You do?'

He smiled again. 'Honestly, Jacqui, you look scared stiff. Am I such an ogre?'

Again her cheeks burned. 'Of course not! It's just . . .'

'I know. You and your guilt complex! Well, I don't think you've been interfering and I do think you are doing a very good job with the children. Even Cousin Adela says so, and that's high praise. No, what I wanted to know was whether or not you like Andrea's suggestion of visiting our neighbours. I wasn't sure if the idea would appeal. It'll mean long drives in the car and . . .'

'I'd love it. I'm just longing to meet more people. I mean if you go to another land, it's not just enough to see the scenery, is it? But. . .'

'Well, Jacqui, Andrea thinks I'm neglecting your welfare. She gave me quite a trouncing, saying I was treating you like a slave, locked up here, and that I ought to show you Australia and not just Kiah.'

Jacqui fidgeted uneasily. 'But . . . but you employed me to look after the *children,* so I don't see why you should have to take me on a tour of the Outback.'

'Neither did I, but I think she may be right. Also she feels it would do the kids good to meet some other kids and get about. Take their mind off their problem.'

Jacqui leaned forward impulsively. 'Andrea agrees there is a problem.'

'My word, she does!' Alain looked rueful. 'I got another trouncing. She thinks I ought to try and get in touch with my sister and find out exactly what's going on.'

'You're going to?' Jacqui's face was alive with excitement. 'Oh, Alain!'

He shook his head. 'Are you out of your mind? How can I? Cecile is two years older than I am and not a child. There must be a perfectly good reason why she left the kids with me. She knew they'd be looked after.'

'But can't she know how it's upsetting them? Can't you?' Jacqui began to twist her fingers together again. 'They go all peculiar if the word 'parents' is mentioned. They sort of close the door and retreat. They're frightened.'

'Now, now,' Alain said comfortingly. 'I think you're exaggerating a lot. You imagine how *you* would feel in a similar position, but

95

Aussie children are brought up differently from English ones. We teach our kids to stand on their own feet from an early date. Sally's well aware her father often has to go away suddenly on business. He's director of several companies. They had a station up in the Northern Territory but sold it recently—but don't ever mention this as the children haven't been told yet. For the moment they have no home, so if Cecile felt she had to follow her husband for some unknown reason, what better place was there for the kids than here?'

'But she could have explained to them . . .' Jacqui began, and stopped as the front door swung open.

Sally came first, followed by Gaynor. 'I think Sunrise should see a vet, Uncle. He's worse than this morning.'

Alain stood up. 'I'll get through right now. Would you come with me, Sally, so you can talk to the vet? You know more about the horse than I do.'

Jacqui saw the quick swift flash of pleasure pass over Sally's face as she left the homestead, close on her uncle's heels.

Standing up, Jacqui smiled at Gaynor. 'Come and play the piano with me, Gaynor. I had an idea in the night.'

They went into the big, seldom-used drawing room, with its expensive antique furniture, its heavy silk curtains and wall-to-wall carpet, and the grand piano in the corner near the window that looked out on to the garden.

They shared the oblong stool and both played, laughing, talking, as their hands explored the keyboard. An unusual feeling of happiness—no, it was something more than happiness, Jacqui thought, it was a feeling of tranquillity, a certainty that everything was going to be all right filled her, as they played.

*   *   *

The next morning she and Sally started tennis. It was certainly an eye-opener. Jacqui's resolve to diplomatically lose was blown to the four winds. She just couldn't win! Sally had her racing all over the court, trying to return almost unreturnable balls. After an hour of it, Jacqui collapsed on the grass.

'You're too good, Sally.'

Sally was trying not to look triumphant. 'We play . . . played a lot. You're just out of practice.'

'I was never up to your standard.' Jacqui mopped her wet face and glanced up to see Alain watching them. 'Come here,' Jacqui called. 'Have you any idea that you have a possible world champion here?' she asked breathlessly. 'Sally is incredibly good.'

Alain looked amused and cool in his shorts and jacket. 'Take me on, Sally?'

Her face brightened. 'Sure!'

They played a tough game, no holds barred. Alain won, but only just. He flopped down on the grass by Jacqui's side and mopped his face.

'My word, Jacqui, you're so right. Sally's amazing. I'd no idea.' He looked at the gawky schoolgirl who was now grinning happily. 'With the right training, Sally, the sky's your limit. Like me to try and get a coach up here while you're with me?'

Like a cloud a shadow darkened her happy face. 'Is it worth it?'

'Of course it is. I'll get one right away. I could do with a bit of exercise.' He jumped up. 'I must go. Work unfortunately calls. Thanks for the game, Sally. You and Jacqui going to practise regularly? Maybe I could join you.'

'That would be fine,' said Jacqui, scrambling to her feet. 'Have we time for another, Sally?'

Sally waved her racquet. 'Sure—the sun's not too bad yet.'

So for the next few days Jacqui, Sally and Alain practised strenuously, Gaynor acting as umpire. Later in the morning, as the temperature rose to amazing heights, Jacqui and the children would go indoors to hear the medical session, the 'Galah chatter', and then do the lessons.

Andrea flew over one day to say everything was under control.

'I've made out a rota, Jacqui, so you'll see quite a bit of this part of the world. Everyone's thrilled to death to meet you, and you'll have

98

to diet quite a lot afterwards as they'll really lay on the food. You're prepared to play tennis?'

'And how! Sally's been teaching me.'

Andrea looked surprised. 'I didn't know she was good.'

'She isn't just good—she's fabulous. Ask Alain.'

Andrea laughed. 'I will. I'm just going along now to seek his advice, but I'll be here for lunch. See you then!' She went, a slender lovely girl in a jade green frock, her black hair a loose cloud on her shoulders.

As Jacqui turned, she caught Sally and Gaynor exchanging a significant smile, but when she asked them why, they both looked innocent. Too innocent to be true! Did they know something about Alain and Andrea that no one else knew? Jacqui began to wonder.

*   *   *

Ruggles called for them the next morning, the huge cream car ready, iced drinks and a food hamper in the boot. The children curled up in the back of the car while Jacqui sat next to Ruggles.

Alain came out of his little house to wish them well.

'Just remember to keep an eye on Jacqui, Sally, and see she wears a hat. It's easy for a Pommie to forget how important it is,' he said,

99

smiling at them. 'Some folks are lucky just lazing around.'

'Come with us, Uncle,' said Sally.

He looked surprised and, Jacqui thought, rather pleased.

'I wish I could, Sally. Maybe some other day. Or maybe we could have a tennis tournament up here. That reminds me—next month a coach is coming up to help your tennis. 'Bye!' He stood back, waving goodbye.

Jacqui, half turning in her seat, to wave, saw Sally's face and was even able to lip-read the words Sally said silently.

'Next month? How much longer?'

Jacqui turned quickly, not wanting Sally to know she had noticed, but her sympathy for the child grew to enormous dimensions and, for a moment, she was angry with Alain. Couldn't he see how terrible it was that Sally should have to suffer like this? Why on earth couldn't her mother have the decency to write to her, to give her some reassurance that all was well?

Ruggles glanced at her sideways. 'Long time no see, Miss Jacqui. How're you liking life out here in Australia?'

Jacqui wondered how many times she had been asked that question. Did the English ask that of visitors to England? She wondered. She couldn't remember, but somehow she had the feeling that it didn't mean as much to the English as to the Aussies, who *had* to have their country admired, they ached for praise, they dreaded criticism. That stood out a mile. Even Sally leapt to the defence of her country over the slightest thing.

'I'm very happy, Ruggles, thanks,' Jacqui smiled, leaning back and adjusting her dark glasses.

The rough earth road wove across the plain of yellow stubble and as the powerful car ate up the miles, so the haze on the horizon seemed to vanish slowly and Jacqui could see the range of mountains there. Gradually, as they approached the mountains, the scenery changed. There were more clumps of trees— strange, macabre trees that fascinated her, like the ghost trees in front of the homestead.

They stood, gaunt and white, their branches extended and leafless in strangely grotesque gestures.

'Ghost trees. Was there a fire here?' she asked.

Ruggles grinned. 'Could be, or else they were killed.'

Jacqui turned in her seat. 'But why?'

He shrugged. 'Trees eat up a lot of water. Probably there was a farm here at one time. You cut a circle of bark off the trunk and the tree slowly dies. It'll stand upright for years, but it's not drinking up valuable water.'

Sometimes they saw small creeks with shallow water and a group of valiant trees. Once as they drove past there was a sudden flutter of wings and a crowd of small birds darted out, to wheel up in the sky, a mass of colour and chatter as they circled and then came together in formation like a display of jet planes. Then suddenly they swooped to the ground, chattering shrilly, vanishing in the leaves, just as a huge hawk swooped down from the sky.

Driving past the body of a dead dingo they saw the crows, huge black creatures with flapping wings and shrill voices, squabbling over the meat, ignoring the passing car.

Jacqui gave a little shiver, and Ruggles glanced at her with a quick smile.

'Law of nature, Miss Jacqui. We'd be wiped off the earth if the animals didn't kill one another.'

'I know, but. . .'

'Don't do to have a soft heart in Australia,' he said. 'You need to be tough to survive here.' He spoke proudly.

A flock of geese suddenly rose in the air, their white wings extended as they flew in a V.

'I wish I'd brought my camera," Jacqui said.

Ruggles laughed, 'Plenty of chance for that, Miss Jacqui. Miss Rank has made a real plan of this. You're going to see a lot.'

'It's very good of her.'

'Oh, she enjoys it. A real organiser, she is.' He gave a funny sort of laugh. 'Only she's not as bright as she thinks she is, sometimes. What I mean to say is, you can lead a horse to water,

102

but you can't make him drink, if you get me.'

Jacqui felt uncomfortable. Should she allow Ruggles to criticise Alain's friend in this way? However, before she had time to speak, Gaynor touched her shoulder.

'Look, there are some kangaroos, Jacqui. I know you're crazy about them . . .'

Jacqui looked eagerly. Further on, there was a group of kangaroos, sitting watching the cloud of dust that—surrounded the car that approached them. Then suddenly, as if at a signal, they all turned with one accord and went leaping away.

She never wearied of watching, fascinated, their way of moving, their bodies leaning forward, their paws demurely in front of them as they leaped on their strong hind legs, with their huge tails behind. It was amazing how high and how far they could leap, and there was a strangely pathetic dignity about their slow-motion movements.

'You're not crazy over that crowd of vermin, are you?' Ruggles asked, his voice shocked. 'Only way to treat 'em is to shoot 'em. More trouble than anything.'

Now they were slowly climbing the mountainside road; half way up, the road wound through a gap in the mountains and then down towards a totally different plain. Here everything was much more green, there were huge ant-hills everywhere, and in the distance, a farmhouse, a huge windmill standing by.

As they arrived, Gaynor jumping out to open and close again the gate in the wire fence, Jacqui saw the excited faces at the windows, and recognised Andrea standing in the front garden to welcome them.

It was a biggish homestead, but nothing like Kiah. Orange and purple flowers grew all over the verandah, but the garden was poor, with very few flowers. A very fat woman in an elaborately-patterned green and blue silk suit came down the steps to meet the car, a welcoming smile on her face as Andrea opened the door and Jacqui got out.

'Here's our new Pommie,' Andrea said, but her voice was affectionate as she smiled at Jacqui.

'Come on, come in!' Mrs. Tadwell smiled, her voice warm and hospitable. 'You kids will find my kids round the back in the swimming pool. You brought swim-suits? Good-oh! Come in, Jacqui. Unusual name—how d'you spell it? How are you liking Australia? Not finding it too hot?'

Jacqui followed her, being given little chance to answer any of the many questions. Inside a half dozen women were waiting; apparently they had driven over from nearby farms to meet the new Pommie!

*　　　*　　　*

During the next few weeks, every other day was spent in the same way. Andrea had organised everything so that Jacqui should meet as many people as possible and also, Jacqui found to her joy, of many different types.

Australia was a land of contrasts, as Jacqui wrote to Mrs. Plaister one night. The homesteads they were visiting were scattered over a surprisingly vast area; some of them were several hundred miles apart, others were as close as ten miles. Often the main road drove through the homestead, and any car that passed was welcomed warmly, offered water, cold drinks and hospitality. As soon as a car was heard, the farmer's wife and relations as well as the children would hurry outside; also a group of aborigines with their small dark children with incredibly white teeth and eyeballs would peer round the building, chattering excitedly in their own strange language.

Often Jacqui, talking to the housewives, wondered if they were as happy as they appeared to be. Sometimes she wondered how they could bear the loneliness which seemed to her to be intensified the more she saw of Australia. Apart from the medical sessions and the 'Galah talks' on the transceiver, many of these women never spoke to a neighbour for months on end. Didn't they mind? They seemed happy enough, contented, busy with their children and work. Yet in many ways it seemed to Jacqui such a restricted life, meeting no one, doing the same job every day, nothing to look forward to except more days of work and loneliness.

Maybe Alain was right and Pommies were different from Aussies, but often she wondered if she could ever love a man enough to live such a life.

She learned how true it was when Andrea had said all stations were not like Kiah. Undoubtedly, although they visited many wealthy stations with luxurious furniture and every comfort, none equalled Kiah, which was quite unique. And some of the smaller farms she saw, when they called on some farmer's wife with hamper baskets of food and merely asked for tea, shocked Jacqui, for some of them were painfully poor, the owners obviously fighting a losing battle with the elements. Shacks with tin roofs and windowless kitchens that must be like furnaces when the temperature was up to one hundred and ten degrees Fahrenheit, yet the women smiled and didn't complain. Some had six children, some even a dozen. Often there were no screens and the flies crawled over them all and the mosquitoes had a feast.

It was a land of contrasts, Jacqui said to Ruggles, as one night he drove them home. The children, exhausted after a day of eating ice-cream, swimming and playing games, were sound asleep in the back of the car.

'I had no idea there were such rich people, or such poor,' she admitted.

Ruggles glanced at her, his leathery skin wet from heat.

'It takes all kinds to make a world, Miss Jacqui. So much depends on luck. Oh, you have to work hard, too, I'm not denying that, but a man can slave for most of his life and lose the lot 'cos of a forest fire or a drought or even the wet. You can never be sure. One day you can be a millionaire, the next begging for a crust.'

He saw her half smile.

'I'm serious, Miss Jacqui. Out here the sky may be the limit if you're lucky, but . . . well, I guess not many of us are lucky as that. I've a pal who bought a bit of ground and struck oil. Now he's living off the fat of his land. His brother, a much harder worker, went in for dairy farming. Spent years building his dairy— then lost the lot through a rare case of foot and mouth. He's penniless, has to start all over again.'

'You don't make farming sound very attractive,' Jacqui said. 'Is that why you don't farm?'

'I'm not a mug. I'm on to a good thing. I like messing about with engines, and the boss is a good guy. Generous too, as I don't doubt you know. I'm putting by quite a pile for my old age. Then I'll buy me a cottage at Surfers'

Paradise and sit back and enjoy life. I'm doing all my travelling now for free—what more could a man want?'

What indeed? Jacqui thought, trying not to yawn. It had been a long hot day. She had played tennis, and, thanks to Sally's training, had done well and impressed her hostess with the fact that Pommies can play tennis, after all!

Suddenly she realised something. Ruggles's words had made her remember that never once had she and Alain talked of money. She'd no idea what salary she was earning—and then she knew it didn't matter. She was having such a wonderful time she would gladly do the job for nothing.

'Land ahoy,' said Ruggles. 'I guess you won't need rocking tonight.'

Jacqui yawned. 'Too right I won't!'

Ruggles shouted with laughter. 'That's good, that's real good. You're even beginning to talk like an Aussie now! '

CHAPTER FIVE

It was a few days later that Alain suggested they all fly with him to see Andrea.

'We've got some business matters to discuss,' he said, 'and I'd like you to see the place.' He glanced at Sally and Gaynor. 'Like to come along?'

Sally smiled, 'Try and stop us!'

Alain laughed, but Jacqui knew a moment of sheer joy. She had noticed how much more often these days he joined them, if even only briefly, and how he went out of his way to speak to the children and encourage them to talk. It was very good of him, for she was beginning to understand just how big was his 'empire' as Ruggles called it, and how hard he worked.

Ruggles, proud and loyal, never wearied of talking to Jacqui, not only about the vast numbers of cattle on this place, the enormous number of bullocks that were sold as beef, but he also talked of two large citrus orchards in Queensland. Nor was she ever tired of listening to Ruggles' accounts of what 'farming' meant out here in Australia.

Alain was still speaking. 'Andrea says we'll have a super sort of picnic. There's a special creek there she loves. Okay then, tomorrow morning. Right?'

'Shall we take our tennis things, Uncle?'

'No, Sally. I reckon it'll be too hot by the time we get there. But swim-suits for sure,' he told her.

They were waiting the next morning and Ruggles drove them across the sun-splashed ground towards the plane.

Alain let the children sit near him and showed them how he flew the plane. Even quiet Gaynor seemed excited, Jacqui thought, and Sally was leaning against her uncle, her face absorbed.

'I'm going to learn to fly when I'm grown up,' she announced.

'Good. Talk to Andrea about it. She learned the hard way. Her father disapproved—he thought women's place was in the kitchen. Now we're going down. They haven't got an air-strip like us, but it's good enough. Watch, Jacqui!'

She did. Now she saw small figures, like busy little ants on the ground below, go racing round and suddenly blue smoke came drifting skywards as some bushes were set on fire.

'That's to show me the way the wind is,' Alain explained. 'Like an air-sock. Hang on, there's a bit of wind, so we may bump a bit as we go down.' His voice was casual and relaxed and the landing perfect.

Andrea was there waiting for them, looking immaculately cool in a pale green trouser suit, a big hat on her dark hair.

'Welcome to Banoon,' she said, and smiled at Jacqui. 'Rather ironical, that. It's an aboriginal word for *sweet water*. It seems my grandfather got lost in the bush and landed up here by the creek. I guess any water would have tasted sweet. Unfortunately every year the creek gets smaller, and lack of water is my number one problem.'

They walked across the dry earth towards a

clump of eucalyptus gums. There was a fence, a low one, and a gate. As they went through, a huge Great Dane came to meet them, followed by a small wallaby.

'Rex is the dog, and the wallaby's name is Lazy,' Andrea explained as the children went to greet it. 'She is—bone lazy. Always sleeping, and does she eat!'

The house loomed up before them. It was the first double-fronted house Jacqui had seen since she left Sydney, a neat box-like house, painted white. The many windows glittering in the relentless sunlight. The garden was also neat with wide beds of what looked like azaleas of all colours, and small weeping willows.

'My garden gets smaller every year,' Andrea told her, rather wistfully. 'We just can't spare the water. It's needed for the grass.'

She led the way inside. It was the first house Jacqui had seen in the Outback without a verandah running round it. Inside it was cool, beautifully furnished with modern furniture and vivid colours, orange, deepest blue, a shocking pink. The effect was bright and cheerful. The sitting room ran the full width of the house, with french windows opening to a shady patio with the roof made of thatch. In front of them was a heart-shaped swimming pool and a diving board.

'Like a swim first?' Andrea asked the children. 'We'll have cold drinks and then we'll drive out to the Greek and picnic.'

It was very pleasant sitting in the shade, watching Sally and Gaynor in the pool, listening to Andrea and Alain talking business that Jacqui couldn't even start to understand.

She half dozed, reclining in the long wicker chair, her legs relaxed, her shoes off. Her eyes half shut, she compared this moment of luxurious laziness with what she would have been doing in England if she hadn't taken Mrs. Plaister's advice. Oh, how glad she was that she had, Jacqui was thinking.

'It wouldn't work,' she heard Alain say.

'We could try.' Andrea sounded just as determined.

'Well, it's up to you, Andrea, but I think you should forget the whole idea. It'll only upset you, and whatever you do, it'll only solve the fringe of the problem.'

'But, Alain, surely even if it's only a small start? Flynn began in a small way.'

'Oh, help, that makes two of you!' Alain was laughing. 'Jacqui is another do-gooder.'

Jacqui sat up. 'I am not! I . . .'

Andrea smiled at her. 'Alain likes to make out he's a cynic. You mustn't believe everything he says.'

'I don't,' Jacqui assured her.

Alain laughed. 'Women!'

'You know, Alain, what amazes me about Jacqui is the way she can adjust herself. Wherever we go, whoever we meet, Jacqui

112

seems to talk their language. Your head would be very swollen if you heard some of the things said about you, Jacqui. You surely are the world's best ambassador for England.'

Alain laughed again. 'Of course she adjusts. She's a chameleon. Isn't that what your friend in England calls you, Jacqui?'

'Yes. She says I adapt to my surroundings. Maybe it's because I had to . . . I mean, when you're brought up in an orphanage you have to learn to conform even though it drives you up the wall. Then with Aunt Elspeth I had to be quiet, docile and hard-working; with the farmer's wife, bless her, I could relax and be me.'

'And here? How do you react to Kiah?'

Jacqui shrugged her shoulders. 'How do I know? I can't interpret my own behaviour. Would you say I'm quiet or gay, studious or frivolous?'

'Frankly I wouldn't know. I don't see that much of you. Hi, Sally!' Alain shouted, and Sally came out of the pool, her wet hair hanging down in streaks round her face, her eyes wary. 'Sally, we're talking about Jacqui. How would you describe her? Studious, frivolous, quiet or gay?'

Sally looked at them all as if puzzled. 'I don't know. I guess she's just nice.'

Alain bent down and kissed her. Sally look startled and so did he, as if he had made some impulsive and unexpected gesture. 'You've hit

113

the nail right on the head, Sally, right on the head. Go and have another swim and then it'll be time for us to go.'

He got up, tall, broad, and strong, filling their glasses with iced drinks, smiling down at them.

'Jacqui is a girl of many parts. Has she read your name yet? She told me I was a five—apparently a very good number to have.'

'Oh, Jacqui, do work out mine. Andrea Rank...'

'Give me a few moments,' Jacqui pleaded, closing her eyes as she mentally worked it out. Andrea would be one plus five plus four plus nine plus five plus one ... then Rank is nine plus ...

'You're a six,' she said finally.

'Is that good?'

'I think it's a nice number for a woman to have,' Jacqui said seriously. 'It means being good at home-making.'

'In other words, a perfect wife,' Alain joked. 'Watch out, Andrea, or Jacqui'll have you standing in front of the altar before you know where you are. She's the world's biggest romanticist and is convinced that without love there can't be happiness,' he said in an amused, indulgent voice.

There was a sudden silence—a strange, meaningful silence that startled Jacqui and made her look quickly at Andrea. Andrea was staring at Alain, an odd expression on her face.

114

And he was looking at her, his eyes narrowed, his mouth a thin line as if he was angry about something. Or, if not angry, concerned.

Andrea was the first to move. 'Come inside and let me show you round, Jacqui. We'll be ready in ten minutes, Alain, could you cope with the children?'

He stood up. 'Of course,' he said, but there was something bleak about his voice as if, Jacqui thought, the sun had stopped shining.

As she followed Andrea round the beautifully up-to-date house, admiring the modern kitchen, speaking to Violetta, the aboriginal cook, going upstairs to see Andrea's beautiful bedroom and bathroom, Jacqui kept remembering that strange silence and the way Andrea and Alain had stared at one another. Was there some secret understanding between the two of them? Were they in love and perhaps prevented from marrying for some reason? But what sort of reason could there be? Alain was an intelligent man as well as rich; surely he could find a way to solve any problem?

The house was beautiful. But it was cold and unlived-in, Jacqui thought, but of course, said nothing. She had a feeling that Andrea was not the happy girl she had first thought her—and then, the next moment, she was scolding herself for 'interfering'. Alain would probably accuse her of 'prying', but Jacqui's natural desire for everybody to be happy drove her on.

'It sounded as if you and Alain were having quite an argument,' Jacqui said casually. 'At least you're not afraid of him.'

Andrea, who was showing Jacqui the greenhouse where she grew exotic orchids, looked startled. 'Of course I'm not afraid of him. Are you?'

'No, I'm not. He's always been kind and understanding, but I was told lots of people were afraid of him.'

'Only if they're crook, Jacqui. Alain is the most ethical man I know. But he cannot tolerate laziness, weakness or lies. Then he does get mad. No, we were talking about the hospital I want to build here.'

'Hospital? That sounds fab, because it's miles from one, isn't it?'

'Yes, about four hundred miles. Actually I want a teaching hospital to give the abos a chance. We'd train abo doctors and abo nurses, and give lectures for the mothers and help them with their babies. There's a high death rate amongst the young babies that could be abolished.'

'Is Alain against it?'

'Well, he is and he isn't. He says the abos aren't ready yet to be doctors, that they need a couple of generations of good education first. He thinks I'm putting the cart before the horse, but one has to start somewhere, some time.'

'What does Danny say?'

'I haven't discussed it with him,' Andrea said, her voice rather stiff.

Startled, Jacqui looked at her. 'Don't you like Danny? I thought you did.'

Andrea looked uncomfortable. 'Of course I like him. He's such fun and yet such a tower of strength. It isn't that.'

'Alain doesn't approve of him, does he? I can't think why.'

It was Andrea's turn to look startled. 'Doesn't he? I didn't know that.'

'He's never said so in as many words, but there's a sort of aura of disapproval when he mentions Danny's name.'

Andrea laughed, 'I'm afraid Alain doesn't approve entirely of quite a number of people!'

She spoke naturally, affectionately; almost as if she had the right to speak for Alain. Surely, Jacqui began to think, there was more than just friendship between them?

'We'd better get going,' Andrea said, but Jacqui had the feeling that she was using it as an excuse to end the conversation.

Downstairs, Violetta was putting a hamper and a box in the boot of Andrea's scarlet car. Andrea asked Alain to drive.

'You know the way.'

He laughed. 'I ought to—by now!'

The children sat in front with him and Andrea and Jacqui in the back. 'We always go there for lunch when Alain comes over,'

117

Andrea explained.

Jacqui, looking round, was struck by the resemblance between this station and Alain's; both were neat, buildings freshly painted, with an atmosphere of hard work as they drove past men working. Yet it was different. Everything looked less robust, less alive.

As if she could read Jacqui's thoughts, Andrea sighed.

'My main problem is lack of water,' she said again.

There were windmills at intervals and the land was not flat, stretching away to the hazy horizon, as it was at Kiah. Here there were many more trees, but not many were starkly white. The creek was about an hour's drive, and as they were going down into a valley, rounding a corner, Jacqui saw huge boulders at the side of the road, then a grove of tall trees through which the track went.

The creek was disappointingly small, little more than the widening of a tiny stream. But there were some low stones near the water's edge where Andrea spread out the cloth and laid out cold chicken and salads, and ice cream from a small portable refrigerator.

For once, it was pleasantly cool, though the flies crawled mercilessly over their skin and an occasional mosquito nipped Jacqui—yet something was wrong.

The gay casualness had vanished. Even the children were silent, eating fast, then vanishing

118

to explore the small grove. Conversation was even a little forced—something Jacqui had never noticed before. Usually they all chatted happily, one taking up where the other stopped. But now it was all stilted, as if each person was trying to do his or her best.

What could have happened? Jacqui wondered. She glanced at Andrea and then at Alain. Was she imagining it or were they exchanging quick, intimate glances? Were they so used to coming here on their own that they were wishing they had not brought Jacqui and the two children with them?

Just as Sally and Gaynor came back there was a wild burst of frightening laughter. Jacqui jumped and looked round. It sounded like a witch's laughter, crazy, even cruel.

Alain and Andrea were laughing. 'It's all right, Jacqui. Only a kookaburra.'

'A . . . a *what?*'

The same crazy laughter split the air again and Jacqui twisted round to look up to where Alain was pointing. She saw a bird with a longish beak.

'It's a kingfisher,' Alain explained. 'You've not heard it before?'

'No. It's . . . it's . . . it's not funny.'

'You'll get used to it,' Andrea promised. 'You don't get them at Kiah because there are so few trees. He's a beautiful bird.'

'A kingfisher?' Jacqui said thoughtfully, wondering if she had ever seen an English

119

kingfisher; this bird looked so big and had such a powerful beak. 'You have some fascinating animals here!'

Sally giggled and they all looked at her. She went a bit red, but explained willingly: 'I think Jacqui has fallen in love with Australia—she finds everything fascinating.'

'It's because it's all strange to her, Sally. I bet if you went to London you'd find it fascinating,' Alain said.

'D'you like London, Uncle Alain?'

He nodded. 'Very much. I'm particularly keen on history, you know, and there, almost every step you take is associated with history. Out here, we're a young, brash country, making our history, so there isn't much to learn yet. Over there, every pavement, almost every building has a story.' He smiled at Jacqui. 'D'you like London?'

'I don't know it very well. The school used to take us on excursions to historic places. I think the one that impressed me most was standing in the Tower of London and thinking of all those poor queens who were executed. I thought of Anne Boleyn and . . . oh, so many!'

'That's what I mean,' Alain explained. 'It makes history come to life.'

It was pleasant, Jacqui thought, the way they were all now sounding part of a community as Alain talked to the children, asking questions, seeking their views. The feeling of restraint had vanished and she could

120

relax.

They were all tired by the time they got back to Kiah. Cousin Adela was grumbling because they were late. After they'd eaten and the children had showered and gone to bed, Alain joined Jacqui on the verandah. She was darning a sock of Gaynor's, her face intent as she bent over it.

'Well, what did you think of Andrea's house?' Alain asked abruptly.

Jacqui jumped, surprised because she hadn't realised Alain had come out to sit with her. 'Her . . . the . . .' she answered, sucking her finger, for, in jumping, she had stuck the needle in her finger. 'I . . .'

'The truth, Jacqui, the truth,' he said, his voice amused.

She looked at him. 'I think the best answer is to say you described it exactly when you called it a house, and not her home.'

He nodded. 'I wondered if your acute instinct would tell you that. Yes, it is a house and it isn't a home. You're right.'

'But why?'

He shrugged. 'I don't think she's happy there. She hadn't a happy childhood, her parents were constantly reminding her of her wealth and of her responsibilities. They trusted no one and tried to make her the same. She inherited this big station and . . .'

'She was telling me about the hospital she wants to build. Why are you against it, Alain?'

121

He looked startled. 'Because it's a ridiculous idea and can only be a dismal flop.'

'But why?'

He ran his hand through his short bleached hair. 'Why? Because a man can't run before he can walk. I agree with her idea, but I think we have to lay the foundations before building the bridge.' He laughed. 'Here I go, talking in parables! The plain truth is this: there are not enough abos sufficiently educated to take on the training as doctors. More abo women or girls could become nurses, perhaps. That's a definite proposition, but Andrea has a crazy idea of having the whole place run by abos. I say it's too soon. It's giving them more responsibility than they're ready for. But that's not the real reason I'm against it, Jacqui. I want her to sell the station.'

'Sell it?' Jacqui's hands lay idle on her lap, her task forgotten. The moths and mosquitoes hurled themselves against the screened windows, the odd moth who had sneaked in was banging against the electric light bulb. 'But why?'

'Because she's very unhappy.'

He began to pack his pipe and Jacqui stared at him, then he glanced up.

'Surely you can see that?'

She took a deep breath. 'I didn't know until . . . until today.'

'Exactly. She's only unhappy when she's there.'

122

'Perhaps she's lonely.'

'Probably. That's why she's often over here. She's found your company very pleasant, Jacqui, though she says you make her feel quite old.' He laughed. 'Andrea happens to be twenty-five, so you can hardly call it old, but, as to me, you seem so very young to her.'

'I'm nearly nineteen. That's not very young.'

He laughed. 'Neither is it very old. Maybe it's your looks—that eagerness, the way you almost *eat* anything new and unknown as if you've struck gold. Your enthusiasm, your idealism, your . . . your whole approach to life, Jacqui.'

'Is it wrong to enjoy life?'

'Of course not. That's the whole point. You're showing both Andrea and myself that somewhere or other we've missed out. I can't remember ever feeling as you obviously do that the world is a wonderful exciting place.'

'Well, it is,' said Jacqui, feeling younger than ever yet forced to defend her own point of view.

'I quite agree. It is. But only people with a certain outlook can see that, Jacqui. We envy you that ability. That's why you make us feel old and square.'

Jacqui began to darn again, her soft brown hair curling round her serious face. 'If she's unhappy in that house, why doesn't she sell?'

'Because she wants to use the land and the money for highly commendable reasons, but it won't work, and when she sees that, it's going to hurt her. Very much.'

'You mean if it doesn't work out as she hopes?'

'Exactly. Then she'll blame herself.'

'Then what d'you suggest she does?'

He lit his pipe thoughtfully. 'Sell the station. Help me build a large school here on my ground—a boarding school. Then in fifteen or twenty years' time, we'll build the hospital. By then we'll have trained enough abo boys and girls to the standard required for studying as doctors and nurses. By then, we'll have arranged for them to have proper training and the hospital will start off on the right foot.'

'It sounds fine, but . . . but twenty years is a long time to wait.'

Alain stood up. 'I'm wasting my time—you're on her side.' He spoke in his usual indulgent way, just as if she were Sally, Jacqui thought, and for the first time, it annoyed her. She was a woman, not a thirteen-year-old child!

At the door he turned. 'I feel like work, so I'll go and get some done. By the way, Jacqui, I have to go down to Sydney next week and I'll be seeing my mother. I'd like to take the kids down. D'you think you can persuade them? I'm afraid they're not too fond of her.'

Jacqui's head went up quickly. 'They think she doesn't like them!'

'As I've told you, that's just her manner.'

'But, Alain, you can't expect them to understand that,' Jacqui protested. Perhaps her voice sounded desperate, but it made Alain return from the door and sit down beside her. His face was grave.

'Why, Jacqui, you really care, don't you?'

She felt herself blush. 'Of course I care. I've been a child. I know how hurt one feels, how . . . how unwanted. Haven't you noticed how Sally has changed since you've been talking more to her? She's always boasting to me about how wonderful you are.'

'She is?' Alain sounded startled. 'Yes, I have thought she was much more relaxed. I put that down to you.'

Jacqui coloured again. 'I might have helped, but it means a lot to her to have her uncle notice her.'

He smiled. 'Thank you. Actually there is another reason why I want us to go down.' He glanced at his watch. 'Time you went to bed, Jacqui. You've had a hard day. Good night.'

'Good night,' she said, but she sat, hands idle, for quite a long time, staring blindly at the moths and mosquitoes battling against the screens.

He saw her as a child, a child to be scolded gently, advised, reminded about her health. But she wasn't a child. Not any more.

CHAPTER SIX

Next day, at dinner, Alain said:

'I've got to go down to Sydney on business and I thought you might all enjoy the trip.'

'Is Jacqui coming?' Gaynor asked at once.

'Of course she is. We couldn't leave her behind,' Alain said. If this had made him change his plans he gave no sign of it, but Jacqui remembered that when they had talked of the trip, he had said nothing about *her* going along, only about the children. 'We can show her more of Sydney as she had such a short time there. We'll go and see your grandmother, too. She's always asking about you.'

Sally's face was sullen. 'Why doesn't she write to us then? She never even remembers our birthdays.'

'She's getting old and isn't well.'

'Some people find it hard to show their feelings, Sally,' Jacqui interrupted. 'After all, she must be fond of you or she wouldn't want to know how you are.'

Sally gazed at her thoughtfully and pushed her cup and saucer along for more coffee. 'You could be right, Jacqui.' She smiled suddenly. 'Maybe we should see her.'

Across the table Alain looked at Jacqui almost triumphantly, but Jacqui was busily thinking of the kind of grandmother who never remembered the children's birthdays! If she truly loved them . . .

The flight down was pleasant except for poor Gaynor, who kept feeling sick but wasn't. As they got out of the large plane at Sydney, there was a cold sea breeze blowing. Ruggles had flown down the day before and was there, waiting with the big cream car. They went to the same hotel where Jacqui had been interviewed. The children didn't say much, but Gaynor immediately went out on to the balcony to gaze at the harbour. He drew in a deep breath.

Jacqui went and stood by his side, her arm lightly round his shoulders as they stared at the liners moving with stately grace down the harbour.

'How long are we here, Jacqui?'

'I haven't a clue, Gaynor. We'll ask your uncle when we see him. Maybe we'd have time to go to the Zoo and also on a ferry to Manly. That's really good fun, and there's a lovely beach.'

'I wish we hadn't got to see Granny.' He sneezed, and sneezed again. 'She doesn't really love us, you know.'

Jacqui swallowed, trying to think of something comforting to say, but Gaynor went on, 'She never liked Daddy.' He sneezed some more.

They went to bed early, and in the morning
127

Gaynor seemed to have hay-fever, because his sneezing grew worse.

Alain took Jacqui on one side in the luxurious room.

'Not to worry,' he said softly. 'We've had this before.'

'What d'you mean?' Jacqui gazed up at the tall man who looked so different in his well-tailored light grey suit.

He smiled. 'You'll see. We'll get the visit to my mother over quickly.'

About eleven, Ruggles arrived with the car and they were driven down to a terrace of houses close to the water's edge. It was beautiful, the trees leaning over, their leaves reaching out for the water. The Heads could be plainly seen and the tall skyscraper of Manly. Although there was a cool wind, the sun was warm.

The house was double-storied with green shutters and white walls, the garden ablaze with crimson poinsettias and hibiscus. A plump friendly-looking woman with greying hair opened the door.

'Come in, Mr. Hollington. I'm glad you've brought the children,' she welcomed them.

'This is Jacqui, who's helping me look after the children,' Alain explained. 'Jacqui, this is Mrs. Webb who looks after my mother.'

Mrs. Webb shook Jacqui's hand warmly. 'You sound English.'

'She is—she's a Pommie,' Sally told her.

Mrs. Webb chuckled and said quietly to Jacqui as they went inside, 'Sally never changes. She was born a rebel and she'll die one, fighting every inch of the way, poor soul. It doesn't do in this world to fight—easiest thing is to conform.'

Jacqui smiled. She didn't agree, of course, but it was wisest to say nothing. Gaynor was sneezing hard, now, and—surprisingly—clinging tightly to Jacqui's hand.

She glanced down at him as they went into the beautifully furnished house and into the huge room with shades over the windows, so that the room had a gloomy look. There was so much furniture that it seemed crowded. Sitting by the fireplace where a small log fire crackled softly was an old woman. She sat upright in an upholstered chair, a white shawl round her shoulders, but her blue-white hair was elaborately waved and her face perfectly made-up, with slight touches of rouge, and even eye-pencil, Jacqui noticed.

'Alain! At last!' the woman said, not stirring. 'I expected you last week.'

Alain bent and touched her cheek. 'I couldn't get away. I brought the children with me.'

'The children?' She sounded startled. 'Of course, the children. Well, what's happened to your manners? Haven't you tongues in your heads?' she said sharply.

Gaynor sneezed violently, and again—

and again.

'Oh, dear,' Mrs. Hollington said crossly, 'I hope he hasn't a cold. I get bronchitis so easily.'

'He hasn't a cold,' Alain said soothingly. 'This is Jacqui West, Mother. She's helping me look after the children while Cecile's away.'

'Cecile? Oh yes, of course. Cecile! So you're looking after the children?' She looked at Jacqui with narrowed eyes, and Jacqui found herself understanding Sally's aversion to coming to see her grandmother.

'Well . . . You look pretty young to me to be in charge of children,' Mrs. Hollington commented as she looked Jacqui over critically.

'She's eighteen, nearly nineteen,' Sally said quickly.

Her grandmother turned and looked at her. 'Well, found your tongue at last, have you? You've grown, Sally, but you're still skinny. And why is your skin so spotty? A good wash night and morning with carbolic soap, and . . .'

'I'll see you later, Mother,' Alain interrupted. 'I have to talk to Mrs. Webb.'

'All right, all right. You come down to see me once in a blue moon and then you have to talk to Mrs. Webb!' Mrs. Hollington turned to look at Jacqui. 'I still think you're pretty young to be in charge of children. Where did you go to school?'

'I went to school in England. I'm English.'

'English? What on earth made Alain engage an English girl to look after Australian children?' She turned to look at Sally again. 'Well I'll be able to tell your mother you're both looking well, but I wish,' she frowned, 'Gaynor would stop sneezing. The doctor's warned me about getting an attack of bronchitis again.'

'You've heard from . . . from Mother?' Sally asked. She had gone very white.

The querulous old face showed surprise. 'Of course I have. Hasn't she written to you?' she asked, her voice sharp.

'Oh yes, of course she has,' Sally said quickly, her face a dull red.

Gaynor sneezed again and his grandmother frowned.

'Really, this is beyond a joke! Most inconsiderate of Alain to bring the boy here, sneezing like this. Well, I've seen you and you're all right, so I suggest you both go and find Mrs. Webb. She'll give you some lemonade. No,' she went on as Jacqui turned away with relief, 'I want to talk to *you*. Sit down.'

Jacqui stifled a sigh and obeyed. As the children said goodbye and left the room, she glanced round. What an unfriendly house! Dark, sombre, cold.

'Now,' Mrs. Hollington sounded more cheerful, 'that we've got rid of the germs, I've a few questions I want answered.'

'Yes, Mrs. Hollington?'

'What is your name?'

'Jacqui West.'

'Jackie? That's a boy's name.'

'I spell it J.A.C.Q.U.I. Short for Jacqueline.'

Mrs. Hollington grunted. 'M'm. What are your parents thinking of, allowing a child of your age to come out here? Or do your parents live out here?'

Jacqui folded her hands in her lap and looked down at them.

'My parents died when I was six years old and I lived with an aunt in England. She died four months ago.'

'So you're alone in the world? H'm. What made you come out here? Looking for a wealthy husband?' She gave what sounded like a chuckle, if it could be so described.

Jacqui's cheeks burned. 'Of course not!' she began indignantly, and forced herself to keep cool. 'Australia is my first port of call,' she said, trying to make her voice sound light. 'I'm working my way round the world. When the children join their mother, I shall go on to friends in Tasmania.'

'I see. I'm glad to hear that. You're young, you see, and the young are apt to be romantic. I wouldn't want you to fall in love with Alain, for he certainly wouldn't marry you.' Mrs. Hollington's voice was cold and crisp.

Again Jacqui felt herself colouring. 'Alain?' Surprise made her honest. 'He wouldn't think of it. He sees me as a child.'

'Good. And how d'you see him? Handsome? Eligible? Attractive? At your age . . .'

Jacqui stared at the old face, now lined with sarcasm.

'I find him very kind. I hadn't thought . . .' She paused. Was she telling the whole truth? She wondered. Had she found Alain attractive? Handsome? Of course he was eligible!

'Good—well, don't start thinking, then. You see, Alain and Andrea Rank have an understanding. It's not generally known, but just after my husband and my sons died, and there was only Alain left to manage everything, Andrea's father and I decided that it would be a good idea for the two stations to merge. Neither of them are in a hurry to marry, but in time they will. I'm telling you this so that you don't waste time feeling sentimental about my son.'

'I thought they were in love,' Jacqui said.

The old woman smiled and for a brief moment looked friendly. 'How sensible of you!'

The door opened and Alain came in. 'Like to join the children, Jacqui? Mrs. Webb's got a cool drink for you.'

Jacqui said goodbye to the old woman, who nodded curtly and turned to Alain. Jacqui was pulling the door to when she remembered she

133

had left her handbag in the chair. She half-opened the door and stopped, as she heard her name.

'What made me choose Jacqui?' Alain was asking. 'The truth is I was sorry for her.'

Jacqui stood still, her hand against her mouth. She tried to move away, but something seemed to hold her there.

'Such a child, and all alone in Australia. Actually it's worked out much better than I expected. The children and she get on well. A similar age group.'

Jacqui gently closed the door and went in search of the others. Later she would return for her handbag.

There was a glassed-in patio and the children were talking to Mrs. Webb quite happily. Jacqui joined them, accepted the glass of ice-cold lemonade and a ginger biscuit. She sat silently. Suddenly she had a lot to think about.

*　　　*　　　*

That afternoon Ruggles drove them up the coast. The next day they went for a cruise up the Hawkesbury River. Then they went to the Zoo and to the cinema later. Gaynor's sneezing had stopped as they left his grandmother's house, and Alain, who had found Jacqui's handbag and given it to her, looked significantly at Gaynor and then at her.

'You'll be glad of the chance to do some shopping while you're here, Jacqui,' he said at breakfast the day before they were to leave. 'Here you are, an advance on your salary.'

She stared at the pile of dollars in amazement.

'Not all that?'

'That's only an advance.' He smiled. 'You've been with us nearly two months.'

Her hand flew to her mouth. 'But . . .'

He laughed. 'I know. You came for one month and then we were going to talk it over. I've been waiting for you to remember.'

'But the time has flown so fast!'

'Jacqui's not leaving us, Uncle Alain?' Sally put in, shocked.

'Oh no!' exclaimed Gaynor, his voice dismayed.

Alain helped himself to more toast and laughed.

'I certainly hope not! I did say a month in the beginning because I wasn't sure she'd be happy.'

'Or that I'd make it,' Jacqui said, looking across the table at him.

They had breakfast served in their suite. Now she found she was looking at Alain Hollington with new eyes. It was almost as if she'd been wearing dark glasses and had taken them off. Everything now looked clear and she found herself understanding many things that had puzzled her.

Alain Hollington was a man, not just a kindly person, years older than herself, something of a father-figure. No, he was a handsome, attractive man. Kind, yes, but he was still a man.

She had never thought of him as a 'man', somehow, until his mother had warned her not to fall in love with him. Then she had realised that Alain was a man.

Mrs. Hollington's words about Andrea had not surprised Jacqui, though the suggestion that Alain would marry Andrea simply because their parents desired it, was something she could not accept. Alain would marry Andrea because he loved her and for no other reason. Perhaps that was why he wanted her to sell the station and then, when they were married, they would live at Kiah.

'Your uncle thought I was a delicate child who'd hate the flies, the mosquitoes and the heat,' Jacqui told Sally.

'And you do?' There was a wary look in Sally's eyes.

Jacqui smiled. 'I do, but I still love Kiah. One gets used to flies . . . or so they tell me!'

They all laughed. 'Well, I'm glad you're happy,' Alain said as he stood up. 'See you later.'

After he'd gone, Sally looked at Jacqui. 'I'm glad, too.'

Jacqui kissed her lightly. 'Thanks, Sally. It's largely due to you and Gaynor being such darlings, though.'

'Darlings?' Sally began to laugh. 'You're the first person to call us that!'

Jacqui walked out on to the balcony in the sunshine. How she loved the view! She could stand there for hours, forgetting everything but the wide harbour with the white sails of the yachts, the ferries happily bowling along.

How glad she was that Alain was a kind man, she thought. If he hadn't been sorry for her, because she looked so young and delicate, she wouldn't have got the job. How lucky it was that he had seen her as a child.

*   *   *

Sydney was fun, especially the last day when they went shopping and Jacqui found herself buying clothes she would never have dreamed of getting in England. She bought Sally a new candy-striped frock and some books for Gaynor. Obviously Alain was paying her a generous salary if this was just an advance! Jacqui found some surprisingly elegant tennis clothes and, as Sally reminded her, they had the Picnic Races to remember.

'Everyone, I've been told, dresses up for that. You must look elegant, Jacqui. Remember you might be the only Pommie there, so you've got to look good.'

Jacqui found a peacock blue silk suit with a matching hat. She turned round in front of the

137

mirror.

'What d'you think, Sally?'

Sally nodded approvingly. 'It's smashing.'

'It makes you look older,' said Gaynor.

'Does it?' Jacqui stared at herself. Yes, the colour and the sophistication of the suit did make her look older!

The assistant, a white-haired round roly-poly of a woman, chuckled. 'I shouldn't think that need worry you yet!'

Then the holiday was over and they were all on the big plane; Alain, as usual, deeply engrossed in his letters and notes. Jacqui had bought a very involved puzzle which she and Gaynor battled with so that he forgot to feel sick. Then came the change, a meal in the restaurant, and then their own plane, and at last Kiah was below them.

'I love Sydney, but it's good to be home,' Jacqui said.

'Home?' echoed Alain, his voice strange.

She was startled. 'Yes, I'm sorry, I did say home. In a way it's the first home I've known. You see, Aunt Elspeth's cottage was very much *her* cottage, and . . .'

He smiled as the plane came down neatly. 'Don't apologise, Jacqui. I see it as a compliment.'

Cousin Adela came to the door to greet them.

'Spent all your money, I suppose,' she commented, looking at Jacqui, who laughed.

138

'I spent quite a lot.'

'And why not?' Alain asked. 'She's earned it.'

But have I? Jacqui asked herself later that night. Somehow she found it hard to sleep. Her mind seemed to be whirling round and round, asking questions she didn't understand, giving answers that didn't make sense.

She slipped on her green dressing-gown and went outside into the garden. The sky—was dark despite the shining stars and there was a round reddish moon. It was quiet, that extraordinary quietness that she had never known before she came to Australia. Not even the howl of a dingo to break the stillness. She drew in a deep breath. *Had* she earned her salary? She knew she would gladly have worked for nothing just for the chance to be here.

There was a small glow in the darkness, then a shadow, which came near her.

'Anything wrong?' It was Alain.

Jacqui shook her head. 'I just couldn't sleep, so I came out to listen to the silence. It fascinates me.'

He laughed quietly. 'I hadn't even noticed it! Tell me, Jacqui, what did you think of my mother?'

She was glad it was too dark for him to see her red cheeks. What a difficult question to answer! Truth was the only way.

'She terrified me. I felt as if she could see

right inside my mind.'

He laughed again. 'Too right she can! I used to feel like that, but lately I've felt sorry for her. She quarrelled with Cecile because she disapproves of Henry, so she's only got me.'

'She wasn't exactly nice to the children, either. She scolded Gaynor for sneezing and she told Sally she should use carbolic soap twice a day and her spots would go!'

'Mother was always like that, but she doesn't mean to hurt. She just doesn't think. Did . . . did Sally ask any questions?'

'No, she didn't, but I felt sorry for Sally. You see, your mother said that Cecile had written and asked her to tell her how the children were. Couldn't Cecile have written and asked *you?* After all, they are living with you.'

'So what did Sally say?'

'She asked your mother if she's heard from *her* mother.'

'And . . .?'

'Your mother answered her very sharply and said: 'Of course, haven't you?' and Sally . . . well, of course she had to say yes. She didn't say they'd only had picture postcards with practically nothing on them. Sally is the most loyal person I know. She'd never let anyone down.'

'I know. Well, Cecile has written to my mother, but it tells us nothing. I read the letter. Simply that she's at the Hilton in London and having a good time. No mention of Henry, but that isn't surprising, as she never mentions her husband because of the things my mother once said about him. It's as if he doesn't exist.'

'How awful that must be.'

'I agree, Jacqui. It isn't easy. Anyhow, Cecile is obviously all right. The letter was quite cheerful.'

'I still think she should write to Sally. It just isn't fair!'

Alain took her arm. 'I know. But there are lots of things in life that aren't fair, Jacqui, and there's just nothing we can do about it. Let's make us some chocolate in the kitchen and then maybe we'll sleep.'

'Suppose Cousin Adela wakes up and find us?'

Alain laughed. 'Well, if she does, it's just too bad. Anyhow, it would give her something new to grumble about.'

In the kitchen, Alain moved round quickly, obviously at home, as he made the chocolate and found some shortbread biscuits.

'You know your way around, Alain.'

He laughed. 'I've lived on my own before now, so I can cope. Did my mother ask you a lot of questions?'

'And how! She thought I was too young and that it was absurd to have an English governess for Australian children and . . .' Jacqui stopped in time, but her cheeks burned as she met Alain's laughing eyes.

141

'You don't need to tell me, Jacqui. My mother warned you not to fall in love with me. Right? I thought so. You're blushing. And what did you say to her?'

Jacqui tasted the chocolate to gain time. Across her cup, she looked at him. Funny that never, until recently, had she realised just how handsome Alain was. How nice his smile was! What dreamy yet kind eyes he had. It wouldn't be difficult to fall in love with him. There was something so alive, so exciting, so . . . what was the word? . . . So thrilling about him.

'I said you'd been very kind to me.'

Alain put back his head and roared with laughter. There was a scuffle and the door opened. Cousin Adela stood there, a long red dressing-gown, that reached to the ground, clutched round her, small rolls in her hair. 'Now what are you up to?' she demanded.

Alain jumped up. He was wearing shorts and a thin jacket. He held out his arms. 'Having an orgy of chocolate, Cousin Adela. Jacqui couldn't sleep and I felt thirsty. Come and join us.'

Cousin Adela looked at Jacqui disapprovingly. 'It doesn't do to wander round at this hour of night in your night clothes, Jacqui. You should know better. Asking for trouble, that's what you are!'

'I couldn't sleep . . .' Jacqui began.

'I know, I know. There's always an excuse to be found. But don't come whining to me one day . . .' Cousin Adela's voice grumbled on as she left them and they could hear the slap slap of her bedroom slippers on the polished floor.

Alain was laughing. Now his eyes danced as he smiled at Jacqui. 'Sorry about that. Maybe I should do the honourable thing and ask you to marry me? What would you say then?'

Jacqui stared at him. And suddenly she realised something. She knew what she would *want* to say—even though it could never be said. It was a startling thought, coming up out of the blue, so as to speak. A thought that had never entered her mind before.

She knew she would like to say 'Yes'.

CHAPTER SEVEN

Jacqui was surprised at the excitement on the 'Galah' session about the coming Picnic Race Meeting until Andrea explained how much it meant to the people for miles around.

'Some of them travel a thousand miles by plane just to come. Lots of these wives hardly see anyone outside their own families for months on end. This is the chance to dress up, meet old buddies and talk. Emphasis on talk! And of course, there's the excitement of betting. Bookmakers fly up here from the cities. You'll be startled by the smart frocks, for people here really go to town on this occasion.'

'Sally warned me, so I bought a new suit,' Jacqui told her.

All the same, the talking and laughing over the air and everything Andrea had said still did not prepare Jacqui for what the Picnic Race Meeting meant to so many people.

The heat was blastingly hot, making her head feel as if it must burst. They flew down, Alain, Cousin Adela, Jacqui and the children. Cousin Adela was wearing an elaborately-embroidered grey silk dress with pearls round her neck and an absurd hat of grey feathers on her head, high heels on which she rather tottered and silk stockings. Alain wore a well-tailored silver-grey suit and Jacqui wore her new peacock-blue suit.

Alain whistled softly. 'That's some outfit!'

'Sally helped me choose it.'

Alain smiled at the lanky schoolgirl in her candy-striped dress. 'You've got good taste in clothes—like your mother.'

'I only said I liked it.' Sally turned away, her voice sullen.

The jackaroos, mechanics and Ruggles had set off in cars and on motor-bikes at dawn. So had the aborigines, piling into the trucks, talking excitedly. Jacqui had been up early to help prepare the food hampers and she went out with Gaynor to watch the trucks loading. The aborigine men got on first, finding the best places, then pulled up their dogs and finally allowed their wives and children to squeeze in. They wore bright clothes, vivid scarlet shirts that seemed to make their dark skins darker. They sang excitedly, obviously looking forward to the day ahead.

As the plane landed on a wide air-strip near the racecourse, Jacqui thought of how much she would have to tell Mrs. Plaister in her next letter.

The heat here was even worse. It seemed to hold a hand against her throat, making it hard to breathe. Cousin Adela put up her white silk sunshade and Jacqui was glad she had a wide-brimmed hat and her dark glasses. Everywhere there was noise, voices, shouts, laughter, so that the air seemed to vibrate. The roads that led to the racecourse were thick with dust as the trucks and cars rolled up in an unending line to park in neat rows outside the course.

It was in a kind of natural arena, a small valley with rising slopes already crowded with spectators as more and more people walked through the entrance gates, showing their tickets. As Jacqui walked with the children, following Alain and Cousin Adela, she saw the people setting up in small groups with folding chairs, tables, and huge baskets of food and drinks. Ruggles came to meet them and said he'd get everything organised. One of the jackaroos, a blond-haired, long-legged boy called Russ, was with him and grinned at Sally.

Everywhere there was this roar of voices

145

and laughter that seemed to move across the small valley and resound back again. But it was a happy sound, Jacqui thought, as Ruggles and Russ brought folded chairs and sunshades and found them a place high on the slopes and with a beautiful view of the racecourse.

Settling Cousin Adela in her chair, Alain turned to Jacqui. 'Like to walk round? And the kids, too?'

They nodded, and the four of them strolled down the slight slope, weaving their way through the groups of spectators. The bookmakers were standing on wooden boxes, large easels by their side as they shouted out at the crowds gathered near them. In the paddock, the horses were being ridden slowly around as Alain led the way there.

'Most of the horses are from the stations,' he explained. 'There's a lot of rivalry goes on, as you can imagine. You won't see any pedigree racers here and no jockeys. Most of the riders are stockmen, many abos.'

One side of the arena seemed packed with abos, standing close together, shouting excitedly.

While Alain and the children looked at the horses, Jacqui was staring at the people around her. Never had she seen such a collection of fashionable and sometimes outrageous hats. It reminded her of pictures she'd seen in England taken at Ascot. Everyone seemed to have put on their Sunday best, and the feeling

146

of excitement and pleasure rippled through the crowds. Many people stopped to speak to Alain and he introduced the children and Jacqui, but then they would drift on.

As they went back to their chairs and Cousin Adela, they met Andrea. She was wearing an ivory silk dress with an enormous white hat, trimmed with green flowers, and she looked even lovelier than usual.

'Alain! Jacqui, how well that colour suits you . . . and Sally, that's a pretty dress, too,' she said, holding out her hands. 'I've been looking everywhere for you.' She chuckled. 'I've just been doing some betting for Cousin Adela.'

'Come and sit with us,' Alain suggested. 'Ruggles can find some extra chairs.'

'Thanks, I'd love to.' Walking with Jacqui, Andrea turned to her. 'Well, is it like what I said it would be?'

'Exactly, only about a hundred times more so.' Jacqui laughed. 'I've never heard so much laughter and felt so much excitement.'

As they joined Cousin Adela she hushed them.

'The first race is starting,' she scolded.

They sat watching. The horses were in fine condition and raced fast, despite the heat. There was one horse way out ahead of the others, the jockey in a bright red shirt, leaning forward. There was a roar of applause mixed up with shouts and Cousin Adela was on her feet, cheeks red for once as she clapped excitedly.

'I won . . . I won . . . I won!'

'Good for you!' a voice with an Irish accent said, and Danny was standing there, his light brown hair ruffled, his grey shorts and shirt crumpled. 'I got here too late to bet. Had to cope with an accident on the way. Everyone's too impatient to get here to drive carefully.' He smiled at Jacqui. 'Well, what d'you think of it? Like a crazy circus.'

'Can you find a chair and join us, Danny?' Andrea asked, her voice casual, but Jacqui noticed that Andrea had glanced at Alain as she spoke and that Alain was frowning slightly.

'The ground's good enough for me,' Danny laughed. 'Where are the kids?'

'Around somewhere and getting into mischief, I don't doubt. Now, Danny,' said Cousin Adela, her voice firm, 'I'm wanting you to go down and place my next bet for me. These stupid shoes make me feel I'm going to tumble down any place.'

'Sure.' Danny was on his feet. 'Can I place bets for any of you?' He smiled at Jacqui. 'Not the betting type?'

She shook her head.

'Well, come down with me just the same and meet a few of my pals.' He pulled her out of her chair, tucked her hand through his arm and walked her down the slope. 'What's wrong with the Big Noise today?'

'The Big Noise?'

148

He chuckled. 'Alain—and who else would it be?'

'Is that what you call him?' Jacqui had to quickly control her anger. She hoped she had hidden it successfully. Somehow she was finding it more and more difficult to hide her new feelings for Alain.

Since that all-revealing evening when they had drunk chocolate in the kitchen and Alain had jokingly suggested he should marry her and asked her what her answer would be, she had found it embarrassing to be near him. She had been startled and shocked to realise that she *would* like to marry him, because it could mean only one thing. That she loved him!

Yet how could she? You didn't suddenly realise you loved someone. Or did you? She had liked him ever since that first meeting when he interviewed her and showed that he found her both young and naive. But love . . .

Besides, he only saw her as a child and not as a woman! In any case, he and Andrea . . .

'Everyone calls him that, but they don't mean it nastily.' So Danny had noticed her indignation, Jacqui thought; she must be more on her guard. 'He *is* the Big Noise around here, but he's a fine man. Yet somehow I didn't feel I was very welcome.'

He left her waiting outside the crowd who were trying to place bets.

It was hot, she could feel the perspiration running down her face. She looked up the slopes to where Alain sat. Round the top were clumps of eucalyptus gums, but there was little natural shade. Was Alain edgy? Or was it simply that he disliked Danny? But why? she asked herself, as she had often done before. What was there to dislike in this friendly, amusing man? Danny was always joking, making her laugh, and yet there was a warmth underneath it all, a sort of strength that came out of it, telling you that you could trust him. Maybe that was why he was such a popular doctor and that even the most ornery grumbling patient did what Dr. Danny told him to do.

When Danny joined her and took her down nearer the racecourse, she turned to him.

'Maybe Alain thinks the hospital was your idea,' she burst out.

'Hospital? What hospital?'

Jacqui's hand flew to her mouth. 'Oh dear, my big mouth again! Of course you don't know anything about it.'

'Know anything about what?' Danny took her arm and led her to a comparatively quiet corner, if anywhere could be called quiet with the voices booming and the roars of laughter. 'Now come on,' he said, smiling at her. 'Or is it a big secret?'

'I don't think so.' Jacqui brushed the flies off her face impatiently. Couldn't they leave her alone for a moment? 'Andrea didn't say so. She simply said that you didn't know about it. I think it's still a dream, only Alain disapproves.'

'And what is the dream?' The race had started, but Danny ignored the cheers and shouts and the sound of galloping hooves.

'Andrea wants to build a hospital and have the abos trained as doctors and nurses.'

Danny looked puzzled. 'And Alain disapproves? It doesn't sound like him.'

'He doesn't disapprove of the *idea,* it's just he thinks Andrea wants the abos to run before they can walk. He wants to build a big school and start from scratch and then in fifteen to twenty years, he says we'll have the abos ready for their medical training.'

'And Andrea? What does she say?'

'I think she wants to start right away. Twenty years is so long . . .'

'I agreed with her. Of course I know she can afford it, but all the same, it's good of her to think of it. Money doesn't grow on trees, unfortunately.' A roar of cheering caught his attention. 'The race is over. We'd better go and find out who's won.'

'Look, Danny, I think I'd better see if the kids are okay and not worrying Cousin Adela . . .'

'All right, Jacqui, see you just now.' Danny waved his hand and strode down the slope towards the bookmakers.

Jacqui walked up to their group of chairs. Cousin Adela was sitting there, talking to two women. One wore a tomato-red suit with a green hat, the other had an elaborate silk dress with a zig-zag red, blue, green and yellow pattern. Both the women were chatting away to Cousin Adela, who was talking loudly. She didn't look up as Jacqui approached and perhaps she didn't know that behind her chair was Sally, waiting to ask her something.

'. . . that's what we always said,' Cousin Adela was saying, her voice shrill. 'He was just a no-good layabout. We warned her, we told her the marriage could never be a success, and it obviously isn't, because that must be why she dumped the kids on us without a word . . .' Even as Jacqui caught her breath with dismay, she saw the shock on Sally's face, saw the unsteady way Sally turned and walked away, her head bent. Jacqui hesitated. Should she run after Sally and say she was sure it couldn't be true, there must be a reason . . . or should she pretend she hadn't heard?

Cousin Adela solved Jacqui's dilemma as she looked up.

'Ah, Jacqui, come and meet Mrs. Gresham and Mrs. Linton. Jacqui's out from England, working her way round the world.'

Jacqui found it difficult, in fact impossible, to escape and sat there, answering questions and of course, the inevitable:

'What d'you think of Australia?'

Inside her, she longed to find Sally, to say she was sure Cousin Adela was making a wild guess, that it couldn't be true. Was that why

Sally had been so moody and sullen? Was she afraid that her mother's behaviour was the start of a possible divorce? Yet wasn't it wiser perhaps to say nothing? How difficult it was to know what to do for the best!

'Are you coming to the Ball tonight?' Mrs. Gresham asked.

Cousin Adela chuckled. 'Can you see Alain at it? By the way, Jacqui, Alain told me to ask you to keep an eye on the kids. They keep wandering off.'

Jacqui jumped up. 'Of course!'

'Nice meeting you,' Mrs. Linton, her greying hair beautifully groomed, said with a smile. 'A pity you're not coming to the Ball. I bet the men would go mad. We women enjoy it, gives us a chance once a year to wear evening dress.' She smiled. ''Sfun!'

Jacqui hesitated. Would it be rude if she left them?—but Alain had given her an excuse. Had he given it on purpose, she wondered, guessing she'd get involved with Cousin Adela's friends?

'Do the men wear evening dress, too?' she asked.

The two women laughed. 'Depends. On lots of things! On how the wife nags, how he feels, etcetera,' Mrs. Gresham explained. 'Aussie men are queer cattle. They do what they like and we put up with it.'

'Why?'

The women looked at one another and

153

smiled. 'I guess we like our men to think they wear the pants in the family,' Mrs. Linton smiled.

Amidst the laughter Jacqui escaped and went to find the children. This she did, finally, and they were in a group of children they had met on their trips with Jacqui and Andrea to the various homesteads. Even Gaynor seemed quite happy, talking to a thin boy of his own age, their backs turned on the racecourse. Sally was in a group of girls older than herself, not talking very much, but when Jacqui went up to her quietly and asked if everything was okay, Sally gave her an angry glare.

''Course it's okay. Why shouldn't it be ?' she snapped. 'We just get bored sitting with her.'

'That's all right then,' Jacqui said amicably. 'I'll see you later.'

She went back towards the group of chairs, but Cousin Adela seemed to be holding court as more and more women joined her to talk and argue. Then Danny was there by Jacqui's side.

'Come on,' he said, and she went with him to watch the races.

In the distance she saw Andrea and Alain, talking earnestly, and a strange desolation filled her. How she wished she was as beautiful and as clever as Andrea—but even more strongly how she longed that Alain was in love with her instead of with Andrea!

Fortunately Danny gave her no time to

think, he kept introducing her to people and everyone asked questions and the time flew by. They all met to have lunch out of the capacious hamper baskets. The children seemed all right and Jacqui avoided looking at Sally if she could help it, for if Sally knew she had heard what Cousin Adela had said, it might only upset her more.

Half way through the afternoon as the heat became more unbearable, Danny, looking at Jacqui's pale cheeks, suggested a drive. 'I'm not keen on the Races and you look exhausted with the noise. There's a National Reserve about twenty miles away. Like me to run you over there? Lovely place, and some strange animals.'

Jacqui hesitated. She had a blinding headache which she blamed on to the intense heat.

'I'll have to ask Alain.'

Danny frowned. 'For crying out loud! Why?'

Jacqui was startled by his impatient tone. 'Well, I am working for him, you know. I mean, I'm supposed to be looking after the children.'

'You're also entitled to days off duty. Anyhow, we'll ask him.'

They found Alain and Andrea down at the improvised grandstand which was really strips of sacking draped across poles.

Alain looked surprised. 'You want to leave?'

155

Danny spoke before she could. 'She's feeling the heat and the noise. I thought an hour at the National Reserve where it's cooler might do her good.'

Alain stared at Jacqui's pale cheeks and nodded. 'A good idea. Why not take the kids along? Keep them out of mischief.' He gave Danny an odd look, Jacqui noticed, but Danny merely smiled.

'Fine. We'll do just that. Come on, Jacqui, we'd better start looking.'

Neither Sally nor Gaynor were very eager to go, but finally they agreed and, once they were in Dr. Mullins' grey car, they seemed content enough. The earth road led the way up the side of a mountain and the air seemed to grow cooler. The Reserve was fenced in and much cooler, for the track went between clumps of tall trees. They saw koala bears clinging to the eucalyptus trees, and some baby wallabies as well as some emus. Danny knew the warden and he showed them round the small tourist-attraction park. Jacqui held one of the bears in her arms and wondered at the dazed look in its eyes.

'They eat the eucalyptus leaves which makes them dopey,' Sanders, the warden, explained.

It was a fascinating place and most of Jacqui's exhaustion and headache vanished. Sally seemed to be quiet, but was otherwise behaving normally. Gaynor was yawning openly.

'You staying up for the dance?' Danny asked as they got in the car.

'No. Alain doesn't want us to be too late because of the children.'

Danny glanced at his watch. 'We'd better get going, then, or we'll be in the doghouse.'

The children sat quietly while Danny drove and talked and Jacqui looked at the scenery. This was much more hilly than near the Kiah homestead; there were many more trees, some huge oaks and even chestnuts such as she knew in England; more little creeks, too, that she saw as they drove by the silvery gleams of water, but still, it was all very dry.

'In a couple of months, it could be pretty dicey as regards fires,' Danny said as if reading her thoughts. 'One thing, you haven't many trees round Kiah.'

'You have bad fires here?'

'I'll say! Terrifying. I hate 'em, especially when it's the kids that get burnt.'

As they reached the racecourse, they saw Alain standing at the roadside, obviously waiting for them.

Jacqui got out quickly. 'It's my fault if we're late, Alain. I'm sorry, but it was so fascinating.'

He smiled. 'It's all right. We're all set to go. I've just got to collect Cousin Adela.'

Danny walked with them to the plane, his hand under Jacqui's elbow. As he said good-bye, he smiled.

'See you next week.'

157

'Thanks for the trip to the Reserve, Danny. I loved it.'

'Good—oh!'

The flight back was swift and uneventful. They were all tired and soon the children had showered and gone to bed. The three adults lingered over their meal, then Cousin Adela vanished and Alain and Jacqui went to sit on the verandah. The moths were banging themselves on the screens and there was a strange humming sound.

'Tired?'

Jacqui looked up. 'Just a bit, but I enjoyed it all.'

Well, not all, she was thinking. She wondered if she ought to tell him what she heard Cousin Adela say, and that Sally had obviously heard and had been upset. Yet perhaps it was all in her imagination and Sally hadn't heard? Or maybe Sally hadn't been upset at all? Wouldn't Alain say she was trying to interfere?

'Especially the visit to the National Reserve,' Alain said. The unusual and totally unexpected sarcasm in his voice startled Jacqui.

She stared at him. 'I didn't say that.'

'You implied it—or at least gave Dan Mullins the right to think so.'

Jacqui caught her breath. Alain was angry. With her! But why? What had she done?

'I don't understand. I just thanked him . . .'

'Thanked him? You practically flung your arms round his neck. You needn't have been quite so enthusiastic about it. Look, Jacqui,' he stopped her from speaking, 'you're eighteen, have lived a sheltered life and are very immature. Danny Mullins is . . . well, charitably speaking, let's say he's got a name for being something of a wolf. He's keen on girls and . . .'

Jacqui sat upright. 'And what's wrong with being keen on girls? Isn't it natural? There's nothing nasty about Danny Mullins. He is not a wolf, he has never made a pass at me, and you owe him an apology!' She jumped up. 'Danny Mullins happens to be one of the nicest men I know!' She turned and without another word ran into the house, down the corridor to her room.

As she passed Sally's door she paused. She thought she had heard something. She opened the door very quietly, but Sally was asleep, lying on her side, one hand under her cheek, eyes closed.

Jacqui closed the door again and went to her own room. She was sure she had heard Sally crying, yet the child was sound asleep, so there was nothing to worry about.

Going to the window, Jacqui gazed out, her eyes misting. Why had Alain implied that Danny was a wolf? Danny was a darling.

*   *   *

159

Jacqui and the children were having their midday meal when Cousin Adela stormed into the room.

'My Bible's gone!' she said dramatically.

Jacqui turned in her chair in surprise. 'Gone?'

Cousin Adela nodded, her face puffy with anger. 'That's what I said. Are you going deaf? Gone, that's what I said. Gone. Taken. Stolen!'

Jumping up, Jacqui went to her side. 'But who would steal it? Couldn't it have got under some papers or something?'

'Of course it couldn't! It hasn't got legs. I always keep it by my bedside, you know that very well.'

Jacqui did indeed. The family Bible was Cousin Adela's most valued possession. It was always kept on the round mahogany table that stood by her bed.

Cousin Adela showed the Bible to every new visitor, pointing out proudly that the first date was 1833 when Mary Hollington, her grandmother, was born in Australia. Her parents had come out from Wales as her father was in the Army. Then, underneath Mary's name came the different names of her descendants, their marital spouses and children. It was Cousin Adela's 'family tree' and if it only went back, in Jacqui's eyes, a short way, at least Cousin Adela saw it as history. But it was of no monetary value. Who

160

on earth would steal a Bible?

'We'll all look for it,' Jacqui promised as she saw the old lady was upset, 'won't we?' she turned to the others. Both Sally and Gaynor nodded quickly. 'We'll just finish eating and then we'll start looking,' Jacqui promised.

'You'd better. If I don't find that Bible . . .' Cousin Adela grumbled as she left them.

'She must have mislaid it. Old people often forget things,' Jacqui said as she sat down again and began to eat the delicious strawberry ice-cream.

'Only when they want to,' said Sally.

Her voice startled Jacqui, but when she looked up Sally stared at her calmly, showing no sign of the desperate fury that had sounded in her voice a moment before.

After they'd finished, Jacqui organised a thorough search. She and the children hunted through the living room, lying on the floor to look under the glass cabinet filled with china, under the couch that was pushed against a wall. They hunted under the cushions and on the verandah. There was no sign of the Bible anywhere.

'It must be somewhere,' sighed Jacqui. 'It can't be lost.'

'Of course it can't be lost. I know that. Someone's taken it, and I'll find that someone!' Cousin Adela's face was a peculiar shade of puce.

That evening Jacqui sat alone on the

verandah. Alain hadn't appeared all day. He was busy, Cousin Adela had said, and was having his meals served in his office. Now, as Jacqui sat there, she wondered if Alain had stayed away because of their quarrel the night before.

If it could be called a quarrel. Maybe she shouldn't have lost her temper like that. Maybe she shouldn't have rushed away. After all, she knew that Alain saw her as a child, so perhaps he was only doing his duty when he warned her about Danny. Why had she lost her temper? She asked herself. Normally she could control it. Maybe it was because she was like a 'crazy mixed-up kid' at the moment, not sure how she felt or why.

Was she in love with Alain? Surely that was the most important question to answer? Why had she suddenly known she wanted to marry him? What had made her suddenly know it?

So many questions to sort out, and somehow she couldn't think straight. First, she had always liked Alain, he was kindness itself. Look at the way he had admitted to his mother that he had given Jacqui the job because he was sorry for her. Obviously he'd thought she was too young to be left on her own in Sydney, and that she would be safer up here until she could join the Dunns in Tasmania. So, out of kindness, he'd given her the job. Didn't that show what a fine, thoughtful man he was?

Secondly, she always felt relaxed and happy

when she was with him. He was easy to talk to, tolerant if perhaps sometimes a little condescending. That was because he saw her as being so young, of course.

Thirdly, she liked this way of living. She was happy. Wasn't she, she asked herself, somewhat confusing everything? Wasn't she reading more into the situation than there was? Just liking someone and being happy with them didn't mean loving them. Why, she hardly knew him. Yet she felt she'd known him all her life.

In any case, if she did love him—what difference did it make? Only that she would hurt herself by letting herself believe it. Alain saw her as a young girl. He loved Andrea and was going to marry her. Now the important thing was that Alain must never guess—never know the truth that she loved him. Somehow she must hide it.

Wasn't it perhaps this knowledge deep inside her that had made her lose her temper the night before? The fear that she might betray her secret?

How quiet it all was! Suddenly she felt restless. Yet what was there to do? Why not have a shower and go to bed? She would write to Mrs. Plaister, but here, too, Jacqui knew she must be careful. Not even Mrs. Plaister must be allowed to guess the truth.

That night Jacqui slept badly. She awoke early, showered and put on jeans and shirt.

163

Passing Sally's bedroom door, she saw it was slightly ajar. The bed was rumpled, no sign of Sally. The children were supposed to make their own beds and daily Cousin Adela descended like a hawk in search of prey into their rooms to see if the beds had been made properly. It looked as if Sally had got up early and rushed out, perhaps to be with her beloved horses, and had forgotten to make her bed first. To Cousin Adela, in such a temper because her precious Bible had not been found, an unmade bed would be the last straw. Poor Sally was not in the mood to be lectured, so Jacqui hastily made the bed and tidied up. In a corner was tossed the candy-striped dress and two pairs of jeans. Tidiness was another of Cousin Adela's rules, and to throw clothes into a corner was an unforgivable sin. Jacqui shook out the dress and hung it in the wardrobe, thinking that Sally's room with its colour scheme of primrose yellow and green was not as pretty as her own.

The dress slipped off the hanger, so Jacqui stooped in the wardrobe to pick it up. Her hands touched something familiar . . . she pulled it out.

And stared at it in dismay.

It was Cousin Adela's Bible.

So Sally had taken it! Hidden it and said nothing. Not even when she saw that Cousin Adela was almost in tears about it!

Hastily Jacqui finished tidying the room

164

and took the Bible to her own room, hiding it inside one of her suitcases, trying to make a plan.

It wouldn't be easy to slip the Bible into Cousin Adela's room without her seeing it, for she rarely left her own room, except to go to the kitchen. She always said she preferred to sit in her room in peace and quietness, and had her own favourite armchair in there. And where could the Bible be put so that Cousin Adela would have to believe she had overlooked it? Not easy questions to answer!

At breakfast Alain, surprisingly, joined them. Sally wasn't there!

'She's gone riding with the lads,' Alain explained as Sarah brought in the fried kidneys and steak. 'Russ asked me if she could go as they're rounding up some cattle.'

Jacqui relaxed a little. At least she hadn't to sit and look at Sally and try to behave as if she knew nothing about the Bible. But how to get it to Cousin Adela's room?

Unintentionally Gaynor supplied the answer. He was sharpening his pencil with a penknife when it slipped, making a nasty cut in his middle finger. It bled copiously, though Jacqui held it under cold water. Then she took the boy to find Cousin Adela in her room.

'We'll soon stop that,' the old woman said crossly as she marched Gaynor to the bathroom. 'Stupid boy! You're old enough to know better!'

165

Jacqui slipped down the corridor to her own bedroom, hid the Bible under a towel and sped back along past the bathroom and to Cousin Adela's room. She had only been there once before when she was shown some family photographs.

It was a cold room, all dark colours. The armchair had its back to the window. There was a brass-topped bed with a sage green cover. Dark walnut furniture made the room even more gloomy.

Looking round quickly, Jacqui stared at the round table by the bed. There were some newspapers on it, and two magazines. Jacqui put the Bible down and the papers over it. Cousin Adela would surely swear she'd looked there, but she couldn't prove anything.

There were footsteps in the corridor and Jacqui looked round wildly. Luckily the window was open, but the screen was down. Hastily she tried to open it, succeeding at last, after a short battle, and managing to climb through the window. She hesitated a moment and then walked as fast as she could down the garden. Glancing around, she saw no one, but she knew she was trembling. It had been a bad moment—there in Cousin Adela's room, when she'd heard those footsteps. What could she have said? Jacqui wondered. Could she have let the old lady believe that *she* had taken the book? Would Cousin Adela have believed her? And if she had . . .?

166

Jacqui walked over the grass, past the hedge of flowers and put the towel on the bench near the pool. It would look natural there, for it was easy to forget a towel.

Then she walked back to the homestead. Well, she thought gratcfully, at least she had saved Sally being caught. She found Gaynor back at his desk, drawing a most weird-looking object, his finger neatly covered with a strip of plaster.

Jacqui sat down and pretended to read, but inside her she could feel her heart still pounding. She was very glad indeed she had been the one to find the Bible. Poor Sally was in a state of upheaval at the moment and a row would be the final straw.

Later Gaynor and Jacqui had a swim, then as they sat on the swing-chair in the shade, they began to work out the song they were trying to compose. Gaynor was writing the words.

'The birds fly high—With their sad cry— The kangaroos hop—Just before they are shot—How dare we say—That life is so gay— so very like play!' Gaynor read aloud.

'It's good, Gaynor, but has it got to be so sad?'

The ten-year-old boy looked at her. 'Life is sad, Jacqui. Things are always going wrong.'

'Yes, but . . .' Jacqui began, and stopped, because Alain had joined them.

'May I?' the tall man, his white shorts

emphasising his tan, sat down by them. 'Did you really make that up, Gaynor?'

'I did.' There was an unusual note of defiance in Gaynor's voice.

'Jacqui thinks it sad. I think it's true.'

Alain looked thoughtful. 'I hate to say it, but I'm afraid you're right, Gaynor. There are always disappointments to endure, disillusionments to overcome. Life's tough.'

Gaynor smiled, some of his tension leaving him, for he had obviously not expected Alain to be on his side. 'Jacqui thinks life is just a bed of roses, Uncle.'

'So it may be sometimes, but I guess Jacqui forgets there are thorns.'

Gaynor began to laugh.

At that moment, Cousin Adela came round the hedge, hugging a book in her arms. Jacqui's heart seemed to skip a beat.

'I found it!' Cousin Adela said triumphantly.

'Found what?'

The old lady looked at Alain. 'My Bible, of course—what else!'

'Your Bible? Of course, it was missing. Well, that's good news, but where did you find it?' Alain asked.

Cousin Adela looked sheepish. 'On my bedside table, under some magazines.'

'I thought you looked everywhere.'

'So I had, Alain. We all looked. It's just one of those things where you look and don't see,' Cousin Adela said testily.

'I'm glad you found it,' Jacqui said quietly, and found that Alain was gazing at her with an odd expression.

'We all are,' he said.

'Well, that's that, then,' Cousin Adela said happily. 'By the way, Alain, Sally's been gone a long time.'

He had begun to pack his pipe and glanced up. 'She's all right. They were going to Maincorn Creek. They took food.'

'She's going to be tired,' Cousin Adela prophesied, and walked back to the house.

Gaynor slid into the water and floated. Left alone with Alain, Jacqui wondered why she felt so ill at ease. This wasn't how she usually felt with Alain. He was still staring at her oddly.

'I thought a day out would do Sally good, Jacqui. She's been looking off colour.'

Jacqui's tenseness left her instantly as she turned to him impulsively. 'It was a good idea, Alain. Help her forget . . .'

'Forget?'

She waved her hand vaguely. 'Well, her . . . well, I think she's upset because her mother doesn't write and . . .

She saw with relief that Alain had accepted that and was not going to ask any more awkward questions.

'I wish she would write,' he said unexpectedly.

'Could you . . .?'

'No, I couldn't,' he said firmly, knocking out

169

his pipe, standing up and diving into the pool. He came up, shaking his head. 'Come on in, Jacqui.'

She slipped off her thin cotton coat and dived in. The water was warmly pleasant, very different from swimming in England, she thought, where the first dive made you shiver.

It was late afternoon when Sally walked in, her jeans dusty, her white shirt crumpled and grubby. She pulled off the large felt hat she'd worn and sank into a chair on the verandah.

'Gosh, it was great!' she said, giving a great yawn. Alain came out from the homestead. 'You look bushed, Sally. By the way, you'll be glad to hear that Cousin Adela's Bible has been found.' As he spoke, he turned away to look at the spring lock of the door.

Jacqui saw Sally stiffen, the blood leaving her face for a moment.

'That's good!' Sally's voice was almost squeaky. 'Where?'

'By her bedside, where she left it,' Jacqui said, not looking up from the crossword puzzle she was doing, or trying to do.

'So . . . so she never really lost it?' Sally's voice was still squeaky. She jumped to her feet. 'I feel mucky. I'll have a shower.'

Cousin Adela came out. 'Be quick, we're going to eat.'

'I'm not hungry, thanks, Aunt Adela,' Sally said with unnatural politeness. 'I'd rather go to bed if . . . if you don't mind.'

'I said you'd get over-tired! Be off with you, Sally. I'll put some cheese sandwiches by your bedside in case you're hungry in the night.' Cousin Adela hustled Sally along the corridor.

There was a little silence. 'Gaynor, I wonder if you'd slip along to my office for me. There's a book on the desk I thought Jacqui would enjoy. It's about the early days when this part of Australia was discovered.'

Gaynor was off and as the screen-door swung to, Alain looked at Jacqui.

'What's wrong with Sally?'

'Wrong?'

'Yes, wrong. I've never heard her speak so politely before.'

Jacqui tried to laugh. 'Oh, she's tired.'

'Well,' Alain stood up, 'if tiredness makes her polite, I'd better encourage her to go out with the lads every day. It's a welcome change from her usual sullenness.'

'She isn't always sullen.'

He shrugged. 'You must admit that she is most of the time. I've never known a girl so full of moods.'

'It's a difficult age and ...'

'And she's worried about her mother. I know. I still don't see what she's worried about. Cecile has a perfectly good reason for what she did, and in her own time she'll tell us.'

'It's not fair to the children.'

'Jacqui, please! There's nothing we can do

171

about it.' She watched him walk away, her thoughts whirling rebelliously. There must be something they could do. Surely if Cecile *knew* how worried both Sally and Gay- nor were, she'd do something about it?

Later Jacqui quietly opened Sally's door. She appeared to be asleep, the thin sheet pulled up over her head, the plate of sandwiches untouched.

Jacqui hesitated. The poor child must be terribly worried, wondering who had found the Bible and why nothing was said about it. Jacqui wondered if she should wake Sally to tell her not to worry—but the little girl had been so tired, it seemed cruel to do so.

That night Jacqui couldn't sleep. She was worried about Sally. Slipping on her thin dressing-gown, she went to Sally's room. As she listened through the door, she thought she heard a sob, so she opened the door and closed it quickly behind her, leaning against it.

At first the room was too dark for Jacqui to see anything, but then, as her eyes adjusted, the faint moonlight showed her Sally sitting up in bed, the tears running down her cheeks.

'Sally darling!' Jacqui moved forward and stopped as she saw the anger on Sally's face.

'Go away! I don't want anyone.'

'Sally, please, I must talk to you.'

'I don't want . . .' Sally turned her head away, obviously upset at being found in tears.

'Who found the Bible?'

Jacqui drew up a chair and sat down. 'I did, Sally, so there's nothing to worry about.'

Sally slowly turned her head, her eyes wary. 'What d'you mean, there's nothing to worry about?'

Jacqui leaned forward. 'Because no one knows. Except you and me. I put the Bible back on the table and . . .'

An odd expression flickered over Sally's tear-stained face. 'You mean they don't know it was me?'

'No—and they need never know, Sally.' Jacqui leaned forward, her hands clasped as she tried to find the right words. 'I'm not going to tell anyone, Sally. Why should I? The only thing that worries me is why did you do it? You knew how upset Cousin Adela would be and . . ."

Sally's face changed again. 'I hate her!' she said, her voice low but unsteady. 'I hate her and I wanted to hurt her. It's people like her . . . saying Daddy is no good, that he's a baddie, and he isn't. He's . . . he's wonderful! It's all Mummy's fault. She's always nagging him, screaming at him. I'm not surprised if . . .' Her voice began to rise hysterically and she was crying again.

'They can't be going to have a divorce. It isn't true . . . it mustn't be true! I'll die if I can't be with Daddy!'

Before Jacqui could move, Sally had leapt

173

out of bed, across the room and out of the door into the long corridor, running along it.

Jacqui jumped up and ran after her, the swinging door to the verandah hitting her on the face and momentarily stopping her as the pain blinded her for a second. Then she was through the door, and through the outer door Sally had left open and into the black night, faintly lit by the pale moon.

'Sally, Sally!' Jacqui called as she ran after the girl in blue shortie pyjamas who was racing over the yellow grass.

Jacqui's left foot got caught in a tussock of grass and she went headlong. It took her a few seconds to get up, rubbing her bruised ankle, but Sally had vanished.

Everything was quiet. The jackeroos and men asleep. The great silence seemed to sweep down to frighten Jacqui. Sally must be somewhere. She couldn't just vanish. Yet there was nowhere for her to hide. This part was plain dried grass stretching away into the distance. Where could Sally be?

Limping back to the homestead, Jacqui tried to remember where she had last seen a torch. Perhaps if she got the key to one of the Land Rovers, she could look for Sally.

And then she realised she couldn't do that. Alain had to know.

But where was he? Sometimes he slept in his room at the homestead, but often he preferred to sleep in his small 'house', which had its own shower, minute kitchen and bedroom. He liked to work late into the night when there were no interruptions, and if he did that at the homestead, he had once told Jacqui, Cousin Adela 'fussed'. It didn't *sound* like Cousin Adela with her gruffness, but she had made it plain that she thought Alain was the sun, stars and moon in her eyes, so perhaps with him she would fuss.

Jacqui limped to the small single-storied house. She saw with relief that a light was burning in the office. She knocked on the door. In a moment, Alain opened it. 'What on earth . . .' he began.

Jacqui suddenly realised she was barefoot and in her dressing-gown. 'Sally's run away,' she said bluntly.

'Sally? But why . . .? Better come in, the mosquitoes are eating you.' He held the door open and followed her into his office. A biggish room with filing cabinets and a huge ebony desk. He pulled up a chair. 'Sit down. Why are you limping?'

She rubbed her ankle. 'I fell as I tried to catch Sally.'

'How d'you mean—run away? There's nowhere to run to, here.'

'Well, she disappeared. One moment she was there and I was running after her, and I tripped and fell. When I got up, she'd vanished. I didn't know quite what to do. She could be anywhere. It's all so huge.'

175

'She can't vanish, Jacqui, so stop looking so worried. What I want to know is, why, when and how did it happen? I thought she was asleep. I looked in about two hours ago and she seemed to be asleep.'

'I know. She seemed to be asleep when I went to bed, but I couldn't sleep, I was so worried about her.'

'You were worried about her, Jacqui? Why? That unnatural politeness to Cousin Adela?'

'Yes, and . . . and several times I've thought I heard her crying.'

'Sally? Crying?' Alain sounded amused. 'Not on your life!'

His indifference annoyed Jacqui and she felt her temper rising. 'She was crying, too,' she said angrily. 'I heard a sob and I went in. She was sitting up in bed, sobbing.'

The smile left Alain's face. 'What did you say?'

'I . . .' Jacqui paused. It was impossible to tell the whole truth without betraying Sally and she had promised not to do so.

'I asked her what was wrong and she . . . well, she said she hated . . .' Jacqui paused, wishing Alain would not stare at her with narrowed eyes like that, wondering why she had been so stupid as to forget to plan what she was going to tell him. If she wasn't careful . . .

She jumped up and winced as she hurt her

176

ankle. 'What does it matter why or how?' she said angrily. 'It's Sally we've got to think about. She's out there and . . .'

'Please sit down, Jacqui,' Alain said quietly. There was a strange new quality in his quietness that startled her. It was so unlike him. 'Sally can come to no harm and I've got to know a few things before we look for her. She's probably in the paddock with her beloved horses, weeping on their shoulders. Now, first, why was she crying? I imagine you asked her?'

Jacqui twisted her fingers together and looked at them.

'She . . . she said she hated . . . hated . . .' She paused. If she mentioned Cousin Adela, Alain would surely guess the truth. Fortunately he, rather impatiently, gave her a chance to avoid the truth.

'Hated us all?' he asked. 'I rather gathered that from the beginning. Why? What have we done to make her hate us?'

Jacqui drew a deep breath. This would be tricky talking, but maybe she'd have the chance to make Alain understand how important it was that Sally's mother should write to them.

'She's afraid her parents are having a divorce.'

'A divorce?' He leaned forward. 'But what makes her think that?'

'She . . . I . . . we heard Cousin Adela talking at the Picnic Race Meeting.'

177

'I see, Jacqui. Well, what did Cousin Adela say?'

Jacqui twisted her fingers again and then looked up at him as he leaned forward.

'She said that she had never approved of the marriage, that he was a layabout and no good and that she'd known the marriage couldn't last.' Breathlessly, Jacqui stopped.

Alain nodded. 'I'm afraid that's the way Cousin Adela sees it.'

'But she'd no right . . .'

'Did she know Sally was there?'

'I don't think so. She was so busy talking I don't think she even noticed I was there. Sally was behind her chair and turned and ran away at once.'

'Why didn't you tell me at the time?'

Jacqui lifted her chin. 'I knew what you'd say.'

For a moment he smiled. 'And what would I have said?'

'That I'd imagined it all, that I was interfering and that it was none of my business.'

Alain chuckled. 'Know something? You sounded exactly like Sally when you said that—a sullen, resentful teenager.'

She felt the hot blood stinging her cheeks. That was how he saw her and would always see her—as a teenager.

'All right,' he went on. 'Sally was upset at what Cousin Adela said. But why was she crying tonight?'

'I suppose . . . suppose it had all built up . . .'

'Jacqui, I've a question to ask you.' Alain's voice had the new strangely frightening strength in it.

'Yes?'

'What were you doing in Cousin Adela's bedroom this morning?'

She caught her breath and felt her face redden. 'You saw me?'

'I did. Tell me, Jacqui, why did you hide Cousin Adela's Bible?'

'Why did I . . .?' Jackie echoed. She stared at him. 'Why did I?' She played for time. Maybe it would be better if he thought she had . . . poor Sally was mixed-up enough as it was.

He leaned forward again. 'Or were you covering up for Sally?' he asked gently.

Again that betraying colour flooded her cheeks. 'I promised not to tell anyone.'

'I see. And why did Sally take it?'

'I asked her. She said she hated Cousin Adela. It was then she said that people were trying to . . . to make her parents have a divorce. She said it was her mother's fault for nagging and screaming at Daddy . . . and she said she'd rather die than . . . than not be with her father.'

'I know she adores him.'

'Oh, Alain, is it true? Are they going to?'

He shrugged. 'How should I know? Cecile would tell no one at all until it was all over, the

179

children last of all.'

'But Sally's desperately worried about it. She ought to be told the truth.'

'She will be—when the right time comes. Personally I don't think it's true, for Cecile loves Henry and would never agree to a divorce. They may have quarrelled and then Cecile have felt it was her fault and rushed after him to try and make it up.'

'But don't you see, Alain, that it's . . . it's terribly bad for Sally. I mean, if she can steal Cousin Adela's Bible to hurt her, she . . .'

'Could do more foolish and perhaps even violent things? Hatred, when you're young, can be vicious.' He stood up. 'Go back to bed, Jacqui, and leave it to me. I'll find Sally. And I won't let her know that I know.'

Jacqui limped after him. 'That you know what?'

'Any of this. I'll simply say that you told me she was upset and had run off into the night and you were frightened for her.' He smiled. 'Don't look so worried, Jacqui. Kids often run away when upset and are always found.'

'Always?'

'Look, Jacqui, she can't have gone far. If I can't find her, I'll wake the men and we'll have a wide search.'

'Can't I come too?'

'No. Bathe your ankle and wrap a wet bandage round it and go to bed. Sometimes you can do more harm by showing your

180

sympathy with people than by ignoring their misery. If you hadn't gone to comfort Sally and reassure her, she might not have got hysterical and run away.'

Startled, Jacqui stared at him. 'You mean ... you mean this might be my fault?'

He smiled tolerantly. 'Jacqui, do stop feeling guilty about everything. It is no one's *fault*. It's just unfortunate that things we plan with the best of intentions sometimes go wrong.'

'I'm sorry, Alain. I didn't mean to interfere.'

He touched her cheek gently, just as any kind man might stroke the cheek of a child. 'There, Jacqui, do stop worrying. Everything's going to be all right.'

She limped back to the house, going in, glancing in at Sally's empty bedroom, closing the door before going to her own room. As she soaked and bandaged her ankle, she wondered if Alain was right—and that he would find Sally at once and that everything would be okay.

She certainly hoped so. And then she remembered something. Alain had asked her why she had been in Cousin Adela's bedroom. He had seen her, probably when she climbed from the window! He had believed that *she* had taken the Bible. Oh, how could he believe her capable of doing such a mean, cruel thing? Suddenly her eyes were smarting painfully. It just showed, even more plainly than before, that he saw her simply as a child.

CHAPTER EIGHT

Jacqui woke with a start and sat up. She could hear voices, the roar of car engines, and she realised that after an uneasy night of lying in bed worrying about Sally, she must have fallen asleep.

She got up hastily and dressed and went along the corridor to Sally's room. It was exactly as she had left it—the bedclothes flung back, the grubby jeans and shirt in a pile on the floor.

Jacqui's mouth felt dry. So they hadn't found Sally! At that moment Gaynor came out of his room, his face drained of colour.

'Where's Sally, Jacqui?'

'I . . . I don't know.' Jacqui hesitated. Should she tell him what had happened?

At that moment, Cousin Adela came to the rescue; the small thin wiry woman stood, hands on hips.

'You fretting about Sally?' she asked in a loud voice. 'She's off sleep-walking, it seems.'

Jacqui and Gaynor instinctively held hands as they walked down towards Cousin Adela.

'Sleep-walking?'

'Seems so, Jacqui. Alain came in late last night to sleep and saw her door open. Took a peep and found she was gone. He's out looking for her right now with the men. He told me she'd walked in her sleep before. Is that right, Gaynor?'

Gaynor nodded. 'She used to at home and Dad always found her.'

'Alain said to tell you not to fret, Jacqui. Sally can't have gone far on Shanks' pony. Come and eat some breakfast. We can't help Sally by starving.'

Which was true enough, but Jacqui found it hard to swallow the food Cousin Adela placed before her. Jacqui saw that Gaynor was finding it just as difficult.

Afterwards, they listened to the medical session and the Galah session. They made no contribution for once, both sitting in an awkward silence. As they switched off, Jacqui went to the window.

The sun was blazing down on the scorched grass.

'She wouldn't have taken a hat . . .' she mused.

Gaynor came and stood by her side. 'I guess she'd find some shade, somewhere,' he said, but he didn't sound hopeful.

'She can't have got far,' Jacqui said. 'Just walking . . . and there's nowhere to hide. I mean . . .' She went bright red and turned to see Gaynor looking up at her. There was no surprise on his face.

'She did run away, then?'

Jacqui sat down suddenly. 'Oh, Gaynor, I shouldn't have said that.' She lowered her voice, glancing meaningly at the door. 'Obviously your Uncle Alain doesn't want Cousin Adela to know, but yes, Sally was very upset and ran away. I tried to find her, but she just vanished. I told your uncle and he told me to go to bed as there was nothing I could do. I've been so worried, Gaynor.'

He put his hand on hers, a singularly sweet gesture, Jacqui thought, as if he was the adult and she was the child who needed comfort.

'It isn't your fault, Jacqui. It's Mum and Dad. Did Sally tell you she thinks they're going to be divorced?'

Jacqui swallowed. His carefully impersonal tone hurt her more than Sally's helpless fury.

'Yes, but she only *thinks*. Uncle Alain is sure they're not. He says your mother adores your father . . .'

'Yes, she does.' Still that carefully impersonal voice. 'Sally's scared in case Dad stops loving Mum.' He turned away abruptly. 'I don't know what we'd do,' he added, his voice suddenly uneven.

Jacqui put her arms round him. 'Gaynor, don't cross bridges before they're built. Sally only *thinks* . . . she hasn't any evidence.'

'Cousin Adela said . . .'

'Cousin Adela was just gossiping like old people do. She never liked your father, but that doesn't mean anything—only that she might distort things and make them sound worse than they are.'

184

'I don't know what we'd do,' Gaynor said again, and he sounded exhausted. He stayed in the circle of Jacqui's arms. She wondered if he knew she was holding him close to her or if he was so miserable he knew nothing but his own pain.

There was a sudden hooting of horns and Gaynor stiffened.

'That's Uncle!'

They were both down the corridor, out on the verandah and then into the blinding heat just as Alain got out of his car. As soon as he saw them, he waved.

They ran to meet him. He was opening the back of the car. 'Try and get hold of the doctor, Jacqui,' he said briskly. 'Tell him Sally's had a bad fall and I think she's broken her right leg. I've put on a temporary splint. Ask him to come up if possible as I think she's got concussion or find out if he thinks I should fly her down right away.'

'She's all right?'

Alain looked at her. His face was wet and dusty, his shirt and shorts crumpled. 'I think she'll be all right. She was conscious for a few moments and knew me. Get cracking, Jacqui. You stay with me, Gaynor, and help. We've got to get this improvised stretcher out without jerking Sally's leg.'

As he spoke several of the Land Rovers drove up behind and the men got out, walking to the car.

185

Jacqui hurried indoors, to be met by Cousin Adela.

'Sally. Broken her leg,' Jacqui said curtly. 'I've got to get Danny.'

'All this noise! Now what on earth . . .?'

It wasn't easy to get him as the girl said he'd gone to the hospital and she was reading out telegrams and messages.

'Tell him it's urgent. Sally may have concussion,' Jacqui said urgently, uncomfortably aware that every family for hundreds of miles was listening.

'I'll do that, Jacqui. Is it serious?'

'We shan't know until . . . until Danny comes.'

'Hang on and I'll try and get him.'

It seemed ages before Jacqui heard Danny's lilting voice.

'What's this about young Sally?' he asked.

Jacqui was about to answer, but Alain walked in and took over, motioning her to keep quiet.

'Sally went sleep-walking in the night and fell into a donga, broke her leg. I've put on a splint. I'm much more worried about concussion. She was conscious for a moment and knew me and then blacked out. I've got her back to the homestead in bed.'

Danny came back on the air. 'I'll be up within a couple of hours, for this is emergency.' He told Alain what drugs to use if Sally came round and her leg hurt. 'Most important of all,

186

don't leave her alone. Let there be someone she knows—and likes,' he added, 'with her when she wakes up. See you. Over and out.'

Alain switched off and sank into a chair, looking at Jacqui, his face tired. 'Thank God we found her when we did. She was right in the sun.'

'Where was she?'

'She didn't go the way you thought she went—she must have doubled back and gone down past the paddocks and towards the old creek. I don't know what she planned to do. I imagine she didn't know herself, she just ran. Then she fell into this donga and twisted her leg. I only hope she blacked out most of the time, for she was in great pain when we got there and then she flaked again.'

'Poor Sally! Breaking a limb's no joke,' Jacqui said, remembering the time when, as a girl of eleven, she'd broken her wrist. 'You told Cousin Adela?'

'That Sally must have been sleep-walking? Yes. I thought it wisest. Sally'll be in no state to be lectured so let's leave it at that.'

Jacqui was going through a difficult moment, for she suddenly wanted to fling her arms round his neck and thank him for being such a darling, understanding man.

'Gaynor guessed, but he won't talk.' She managed to keep her voice steady and to sit still.

Alain stood up. 'Nothing more we can
187

do. Would you sit with Sally until the doctor comes? I'll have a shower and something to eat and come along to see how she is.'

'Can Gaynor sit with me?'

Alain looked surprised. 'I don't see why not, but . . .'

'He's pretty upset, too, and it'd be better than to let him sit alone.'

'All right. Just keep quiet and be by her side if she wakes up.'

Jacqui nodded. She went and collected some sewing, some papers to read, and Gaynor. She found him alone on the verandah, just as pale, staring out at the sun-scorched world.

'Gaynor, Uncle Alain has asked me to sit with Sally in case she wakes up. Would you keep me company?'

He swung round. 'All right.'

'Get some books or something. It may be quite a while before Danny gets here.'

Sally was unconscious, lying on top of the bed, in the same crumpled blue shortie pyjamas, one leg strapped to a long piece of wood. Her face was covered with red crust, her hair a tangled mess, and a sheet was laid over her. Jacqui longed to wash the poor dusty face, but she hesitated. Maybe it would be better to wait until Danny came. Perhaps if they moved Sally, more damage could be done.

She and Gaynor sat down by the bed and Cousin Adela brought them long glasses of iced orange squash. She tiptoed out, glancing compassionately at Sally.

Jacqui kept her eyes on the book she was pretending to read and wondered what Cousin Adela would say if she knew that her careless, malicious words at the Picnic Race Meeting had triggered off this trouble. It was so easy to talk without thinking, perhaps without ever knowing the harm that had been done.

They heard a plane circling overhead. Gaynor jumped up and went off to reconnoitre. He came back and said it wasn't the doctor, it was Andrea.

It seemed ages before Andrea walked in, looking delightfully cool in her leaf-green trouser suit.

'Poor Sally! Alain was telling me,' Andrea said softly. 'No sign of consciousness?'

Jacqui shook her head. 'Danny's on his way.'

'I know. I heard it on the air. Look, Jacqui, suppose you and Gaynor go and relax for a while. I'll sit here with Sally.'

Jacqui hesitated. Danny had said that someone Sally knew and liked must sit with her. Did Sally like Andrea? Yet, Jacqui thought, she could hardly refuse Andrea's offer.

'Thanks.' She stood up.

'I'm staying here,' Gaynor said gruffly.

Jacqui touched his shoulder lightly. 'All right. I'll just go and stretch my limbs.'

'Have a rest, Jacqui,' Andrea told her. 'Danny may need your help.'

'My help? Why my help?'

Andrea smiled ruefully. 'I'm no good when anyone's ill. Once I helped Danny with quite a small emergency op. and I flaked out. Since then he won't have me anywhere near a patient.'

'You couldn't help it,' Jacqui smiled. 'Send Gaynor for me if you need me. I'll be in my room.'

She had made what might be called an 'instant decision'. She knew what she was going to do and she would do it without hesitation. But Alain mustn't know. Nor Andrea or Cousin Adela. Danny would understand. Danny was different. He didn't believe in this family's refusal to become involved, to leave others to work out their own problems.

It was a difficult letter to write. Jacqui tore up four attempts and wasn't even very happy about the fifth, but time was running out and she must have it ready. Finally she sat back and read what she had written. 'Dear Mrs. Tonkin,' it began, 'I hope you won't think I am interfering, but I feel you ought to know that both Sally and Gaynor are very worried about things. I know Alain will be angry with me for writing to you because he says you know what you are doing and we have no right to interfere. But I think you ought to be told

190

that Sally and Gaynor think that you and your husband are going to have a divorce and they are both most frightfully upset. Sally shows it more, but both are very worried. They can't understand why you left them here without saying anything, and people are talking. Sally got so upset she ran away last night, fell into a donga and broke her leg. We are waiting for the doctor as we think it may be concussion. Please, please, Mrs. Tonkin, write to Sally and tell her why you went to London so that she can stop worrying about it. I'm sorry if you think I am interfering, but I am very fond of Sally and Gaynor and I want them to be happy.'

She read the letter again and wondered how Cecile Tonkin would react. Would she crumple the letter and throw it away?

Luckily Jacqui had stamps and an air-mail envelope. Hastily she addressed it to the Hilton Hotel and added: 'Please forward'. She didn't put the homestead's postal address on the back of the envelope, as she didn't want it to come back. She put on a pale blue dress with pockets and tucked the letter in, and heard the roar of a plane circling overhead as she hurried out.

Andrea was at Sally's door. She shook her head when Jacqui looked at her. 'No, she didn't even flutter her eyelids.'

Danny came briskly, his bag in one hand, Alain close behind. Danny looked tired, red

191

dust on his pale grey shorts and shirt.

'No change? Come in with me, Jacqui.' He smiled at Andrea. 'No offence meant!'

Andrea smiled back. 'None taken. I was telling Jacqui I'm a weakling.'

'We all have our Achilles' heel,' he said.

He asked Gaynor to go and the small boy left reluctantly. Jacqui stood quietly while Danny got to work.

It seemed a long time before he stopped examining the unconscious girl and straightened.

'Well?'

He shrugged. 'Difficult to tell. I'll have to fly her down to the hospital. We'll need X-rays and tests. Tell me what happened.'

Jacqui hesitated. There were the two stories.

Danny frowned. 'I want the truth, Jacqui. Not Alain's crazy nonsense about the child walking in her sleep.'

'He said that to protect Sally. He didn't want Cousin Adela to scold her. You see, Danny, Sally's very unhappy.' Quickly, her voice low, Jacqui told Danny everything— about Sally's moods, her disinclination to mention or talk of her parents, the overheard conversation at the Picnic Race Meeting, the disappearance of Cousin Adela's Bible.

'That was when I really got worried,' Jacqui confessed. 'I know that when they're emotionally disturbed children start stealing.'

'What reason did she give?'

'She said she hated Cousin Adela. That it was lies. She defended her father loyally. She adores him. She said people said there would be a divorce. She got quite hysterical, started to cry again and suddenly rushed out of the room.'

Jacqui described how she had tried to catch Sally, how she had fallen, and, in the end, gone to Alain.

'He told me to go to bed and he went searching. It was a long time before they found her. Now you know it all. Danny, I need your help.' Jacqui moved closer to Danny, her voice little more than a whisper. 'Alain refuses to tell his sister how upset Sally has been. Of course he'll have to tell her about *this*, but I know he won't tell her the reason it happened. You see, Danny, Alain thinks I'm a do-gooder, that I interfere too much, even with the best of intentions, and he says this is his sister's business and he has no right to interfere.'

'And you don't agree.'

'No, I don't. I think his sister has the right to know the truth, that the children think the marriage is breaking up and are very upset.'

'And suppose the marriage *is* breaking up?'

'Well, isn't it better to know the worst than to keep fearing it? Alain doesn't think they are. He says his sister adores her husband and would never consider a divorce. But I'm worried about Sally, Danny.'

193

'So am I. What you've told me explains a lot.' He took the letter and stared down at it. 'You know, Alain will be furious when he discovers this.'

'I know.' Jacqui lifted her chin. 'It can't be helped. I've got to do something, someone has to, and . . . I don't want to get *you* into trouble, Danny.'

He grinned. 'I'm not scared. I agree with you. She should be told, otherwise Sally's whole life may be affected by the emotional disturbance from which she is suffering. Poor little brat!' he added, gazing down at the unconscious girl. 'Well, I'll post the letter right away, Jacqui, and try not to worry. I think Sally'll be all right.'

Jacqui followed him outside to where Andrea and Alain were talking. 'She'd better come down to the hospital with me,' Danny said curtly. 'I need X-rays and certain tests. The sooner we're away the better.'

'Shall I come with you?' Andrea asked.

Danny looked startled. 'No, I don't need help. Sally's unconscious and I've given her an injection so she won't wake up.'

'I don't mind coming,' said Andrea.

Danny smiled. 'I know. Thanks. But it only constitutes the problem of getting you home. I'll get the stretcher.'

Jacqui felt a small damp hand slide into hers. She glanced down and Gaynor was by her side.

194

'Is she going to be all right?'

Jacqui nodded. 'Of course. The doctor just wants to take X-rays and things before putting her leg in plaster. Everything's going to be all right, Gaynor.'

They watched in silence as two of the mechanics carried out the stretcher. Sally's head lolled to one side, her eyes closed.

There was a moment of stillness after the plane had taken off and circled. They watched it become a small speck in the cloudless sky.

Andrea spoke first. 'I don't know about you folk, but I'm starving.' She turned to the silent, small old woman. 'Will I be an awful nuisance?'

Cousin Adela looked at her coldly. Jacqui realised something she had not realised before. Cousin Adela not only disapproved of Andrea, but disliked her! Why? Then the answer became clear and Jacqui knew sympathy for old Cousin Adela, happily installed as queen of Kiah, and afraid that Alain would marry Andrea, and Cousin Adela would become redundant and have to find a new home. Sympathy, too, for Andrea, who didn't deserve the hostility and certainly had never consciously done anything to make the old lady dislike her! How complicated life became when you fell in love, Jacqui thought. If only . . .

And then she knew that perhaps her problem would soon be solved. Once Cecile

Tonkin had the letter, it was quite possible she would fly out and collect the children, to prove that the rumour was a pack of lies. Once the children had gone, Jacqui would be *redundant*. Alain would pay her generously and her air-flight to Sydney and she would be two thousand miles from him. Surely once she no longer saw him every day, she could fight and overcome this love she felt for him? It was just that it was so hard, being so near him, and yet so far.

'There's a cold meal waiting for any who likes it,' Cousin Adela was saying grumpily, so they all went inside.

Andrea tried to make the gathering gay, but she failed, for the laughter was forced and there were long awkward pauses in which no one said anything. Jacqui could not forget poor Sally, running, the tears rolling down her cheeks, as she faced her fear. Supposing there was a divorce? Who would have the children? Poor Sally, angry, hurt and frightened, running away from something that would pursue her, no matter where she went. Then Jacqui thought of the letter in Danny's pocket and she knew an uprising of hope. Surely any mother worthy of the name would react at once?

But, apparently, things seldom worked out as expected. Days passed and Danny talked on the air, telling them that Sally had not had concussion, but it was largely shock and a broken leg. As soon as he deemed it wise,

196

she could go home. Andrea flew over quite often and chatted with Jacqui. Jacqui tried to keep Gaynor happy, but he had retreated into his shell of indifference again, rarely talking, hiding behind a book without turning the pages. It worried Jacqui.

She tried to talk to Alain about it.

'Of course he's upset,' Alain agreed. 'He's very dependent on Sally.'

'You wrote and told . . .'

'My sister? Of course.' Alain smiled. 'Really, Jacqui, you do fuss!'

'But she's not answered?'

He shrugged. 'She may be away. I sent it to the Hilton. Look, Jacqui, try to keep calm. Sally's in no danger at all. Every day she's better. Soon she'll be home.'

'Home?'

Alain stood up. 'I know it isn't her real home, Jacqui, but it's the next best thing.'

Perhaps that was why there had been no answer to her letter, Jacqui thought. Perhaps Sally's mother was no longer at the Hilton Hotel. Perhaps she knew nothing about it . . . Was there nothing they could do?

Sally came home, a subdued, quiet Sally who spent most of her time lying on the couch, eyes half closed. Her leg was heavy with plaster. She had migraines for which Danny gave her pills. She was polite but withdrawn, rarely laughing. Cousin Adela thought it a great improvement.

Jacqui told Alain it was breaking her heart.

'It isn't natural. Can't you see that? Sally's still terribly worried.'

'I do see that, but what can we do about it? We can only take care of her.'

'Take care of her body, perhaps, but not her heart,' Jacqui said, and walked out of the room.

Later she apologised to Alain. He put his arm round her shoulder, just as she had seen him often do with Sally.

'My poor little Jacqui,' he said in that infuriatingly condescendingly kind voice. 'You mustn't get so involved. It won't help Sally, because she'll sense your tension.'

'I can't help it. If only her mother . . .' Jacqui put her hand up to her mouth to steady her suddenly trembling lips, for she was near tears. 'If only her mother would write!'

One day the mail came. Cousin Adela liked to sort it out and no one was allowed to have letters until the sorting was done.

'Ah!' said Cousin Adela, making three piles on the verandah table. 'A letter for Sally!'

Sally, sprawled on the couch, didn't look up as Cousin Adela put it on the side. 'Letters for Jacqui and a pile for Alain. Nothing for Gaynor, nor for me.'

Jacqui's hands were trembling as she sorted out her letters, for there were three from Mrs. Plaister, one from the farmer's wife, and one . . . had a London postmark! Jacqui gathered the letters to go to her room. Alain, sorting out his letters, looked up.

'Aren't you going to read your letter, Sally? Looks like your mother's writing.'

It was hot today in the verandah, but suddenly Jacqui shivered. Sally half sat up, put out her hand for the envelope and tried to open it.

'Let me,' said Jacqui, putting down her letters. She opened the envelope in a moment and gave it to Sally. Sally had gone very white. Her face looked thin, the cheek bones protruding, her eyes sunk.

'You read it, Jacqui.'

Jacqui looked across the room at Alain. He nodded. She unfolded the paper and began to read.

'My dearest Sally and Gaynor, I was upset to hear you had hurt your leg, Sally, and hope you are better. I've been meaning to write to you both for a long time, but I was too worried. You see . . .' Jacqui's voice was slightly unsteady as she tried to read ahead as well as read the words she was saying, 'I have been very worried about Daddy. We never told you, but he has been ill for months. I tried to make him see a doctor, but he refused. Then he fainted at the office and they sent for a doctor. He learned he had to have an operation that could only be done in London. That's why we couldn't go to New Zealand, Gaynor, this year. Daddy didn't want you to know, so he went to London alone, but I was so worried about him that I had to go too. I've often thought I should have told you, Sally, and Gaynor too, but I knew how frightened and upset you would be. That was why I took you to Kiah. I know I should have told you, but I hadn't the courage. I was afraid for Daddy, myself. I'm glad to say he's had the operation and everything is all right. He sends his love and will write to you next week. We hope to fly back in about two months' time, so please ask Uncle Alain if you can stay on. I'll be writing to you now often. I couldn't write before because I was so worried. We'll all go to New Zealand next year, Gaynor, so try to forgive us for something that wasn't our fault.'

Jacqui put down the letter and smiled at Sally. 'She sends hugs and kisses to you both.'

'Daddy *is* all right?' Sally sounded shocked.

'Yes. She says he'll write next week, so he must be all right.'

'I wish she'd told us!'

'She didn't want you to worry.'

Sally smiled ruefully. 'I guess not.'

Jacqui handed her the letter. 'Here you are. You've got her address now, so you can both write to her. I expect she's longing to hear how you are.'

Jacqui went to pick up her letters and saw, with a shock, that the letter with the London postmark was on top. Had she left it on top or . . .?

She glanced at Alain, who was talking to Sally. Jacqui hurried to her room. She tore open the letter from London. It was short and, somehow, right.

'*Dear Jacqui, Thank you so much. Thank you so very much. Looking forward to meeting you one day,*' she read. It was signed, '*Cecile Tonkin*'.

There was a sharp knock on the door. Jacqui hurriedly thrust the letter into her pocket as she called, 'Who is it?'

The door opened and Alain stood there. He came into the room, closing the door behind him.

'You heard from my sister.'

It was more of a statement than a question and she knew he must have seen the envelope.

Now she was for it, Jacqui thought, but she lifted her pointed chin and faced him.

'I did.'

'And what did she say?'

Jacqui pulled out the letter, straightened the crumpled sheet, and handed it to him.

He read it silently and handed it back. 'Where did you get the address?'

'You gave it to me . . . or was it Andrea? I know someone told me your sister always stayed at the Hilton in London,' Jacqui said, bracing herself for the storm she knew was coming.

'How did you post it?' Alain asked. An appropriate question, for any letters for the mail were always put on an antique silver salver in the lounge and collected from there. Had Jacqui put her letter with the others, it was almost certain it would have been seen.

Jacqui drew a deep breath. 'I got . . . got someone to post it for me.'

Alain stared at her. 'I see. That someone can only be Danny Mullins. I'm sorry you felt you could trust Danny rather than me.' He turned away, his hand on the door handle.

'Alain, that isn't fair!' Jacqui said at once. 'You know how often I've asked you to write to your sister.'

'I know. It happens that I was wrong and you were right,' Alain told her, his voice quiet. 'All the same, I didn't realise that Danny meant so much to you.'

He opened the door, went out and closed it behind him. Jacqui stood staring at the closed door for a long moment. Then her shoulders dropped and she sat down, feeling surprisingly exhausted. So Alain believed she was in love with Danny!

She sighed. Maybe it was just as well. Then he could never discover the truth; that she loved him.

CHAPTER NINE

What a difference her mother's letter had made to Sally, Jacqui thought. She was a different girl, relaxed and able to talk about her parents now that her fear had gone. She began to tease Gaynor, to ask Jacqui to play cards with her. Often she talked of her father, reminding Gaynor that they had noticed their father had lost a lot of weight.

'I wonder what's wrong with him. It must be something pretty serious if he had to go to London to be operated on.'

Danny, who had come out to take his clinic, shook his head. 'Not necessarily, Sally. There are some surgeons who've made names for themselves for individual and often original operations. I should say it could have been something to do with his kidneys. You did say once his legs were swollen?'

Sally nodded.

'Many men as they grow older have kidney trouble, but nowadays it can be handled quite well, so not to worry. Anyhow, he'll be back out here in two months.'

Even Cousin Adela seemed satisfied with Cecile's letter.

'Poor girl, she must have been worried stiff,' the little old lady commented. 'No wonder she dashed off like that. She must have dreaded being asked questions. Anyhow, it's good news your father's had his op and all is well. Now it's just a matter of being patient. Two months will soon go.'

Indeed it will, Jacqui thought, looking out through the screened windows towards the ghost trees. They stood like tragic sentinels, their stark white branches outspread, the wiry twigs pointing like a witch's fingers. Two months would soon go, and her services would no longer be needed. She would leave Kiah and fly back to Sydney; perhaps even go on to Tasmania, for Kay Dunn had written from there to say she had joined her husband as he had found them a house.

In two months' time, Jacqui told herself, this strangely fascinating life—that seemed so completely different from life as she had known it—would be over. She would become just a name that Andrea or Alain might casually mention, hardly a memory worth keeping. But she would never forget Alain. Never so long as she lived. Nor would she want to.

Andrea flew over to see Alain, and Jacqui and the children watched her small white plane land neatly. They saw Alain walk out of one of the hangars to talk to her; later they saw the two of them go into Alain's little house.

'D'you think Andrea . . .' Gaynor began, but Sally kicked him with her free foot.

'I want to talk to Andrea about learning

to fly. I don't know how old you've got to be. Would you like to learn to fly, Jacqui?'

'What? Oh!' Jacqui's thoughts had been far away as she pictured Alain taking Andrea into his arms, after they had closed the door on the outside world. She could imagine how he would hold Andrea, his arms tight, his mouth hard on hers. 'What did you say, Sally? Oh, yes, would I like to fly?'

'Yes.'

'I don't know. If I lived here, I think I would, but I'm not sure I'd like to fly in England. Too many jets about.'

'Will you go back to England? I mean, when we go home?'

Jacqui hesitated. 'Honestly, Sally, I don't know. You see, I haven't any real family there. Mrs. Plaister, of course, the Vicar's wife, was marvellous to me, but she's not really 'family'. I think that now I've started going round the world, I'll go on with it.'

'Where will you go first?'

'Where, Gaynor? Well, maybe I'll have a week or two in Sydney. I'd like to visit the Blue Mountains, and go up the Hawkesbury River . . . maybe I'd go to the Gold Coast to see your lovely beaches. I'd also like to see Alice Springs and I'd like to go to the Barrier Reef. It's so difficult. There are so many wonderful things to see here, but it all costs money. Maybe I'll get a job in Sydney and save hard so that I can see all these places and then,

205

afterwards, go on to Tasmania. I've also got addresses in New Zealand. I'd like to go there, and Mrs. Plaister has a cousin in Fiji, so I might go there too.'

Sally sighed. 'It sounds gorgeous. I can't wait to be grown up.'

The car drew up outside, Ruggles jumped out to open the door for Andrea. Andrea, looking lovelier than ever in her white dress and big green hat. She came up the steps with her usual graceful movements.

'Sally, I am sorry to hear your father's been so ill. Your uncle tells me everything's all right now, though?'

'Oh yes,' Sally said cheerfully. 'They're coming back in two months' time.'

'That'll be marvellous. How's the leg? Oughtn't we to autograph your plaster cast?'

Sally giggled, 'I never thought of that!' She held out her leg while Andrea, Jacqui and Gaynor all solemnly signed their names.

Gaynor was struggling with a jigsaw puzzle. 'I'm sure there's a piece missing,' he said.

'Let me see,' Sally told him. 'It needs brains!'

'I bet you six cents you can't find it,' Gaynor said as he carried the tray to put it on the table by Sally's side.

Andrea laughed gently. 'Looks like we're redundant, Jacqui. Let's take a cup of coffee in the garden. I want to talk to you.'

They sat, Jacqui curled up on the swing

206

chair, Andrea lying gracefully in the long, cushioned wicker chair, her hat pushed back, as she looked thoughtfully at Jacqui, in her simple blue dress.

'I'd have posted that letter for you if you'd asked me, Jacqui.'

'Alain told you?'

'Of course. I was on your side, Jacqui. Alain was . . .'

'Angry with me, I know! I knew he would be.' Jacqui tucked her feet under her. 'That's why I didn't tell him. Maybe I should have talked to you and you could have talked him into it.'

Andrea laughed. 'Are you crazy? No one can talk Alain into anything! Not even me. We don't always see eye to eye, you know. I must say, though, Jacqui, there's one thing I love about Alain. If he's wrong, he's got the courage to admit it. Now he says you did the right thing in writing to Cecile and that he was wrong. Not many men would admit that.'

'I know.' Jacqui looked down at her hands, her fingers entwined. 'I know. Alain is a most unusual man.' She could not look up; she was afraid Andrea would recognise the truth in her eyes.

Andrea drank some coffee. There were the usual noises—distant shouts, the roar of a motor-bike, laughter, the sound of galloping hooves from the distance.

'You really are happy here, Jacqui?'

'Of course.'

'I mean, living in Australia and the Outback?'

Startled, Jacqui looked up and saw that Andrea was looking uneasy. 'Why, yes. I like this way of living.'

'Life in Australia isn't always as gracious as it is here, Jacqui. Being wealthy makes a difference. You've seen some of the less fortunate farms. Could you live like those women?'

Jacqui frowned. 'Frankly, I don't know. I've often thought of that myself, but I suppose if you love someone enough . . .'

'That's just the point. Do you?'

Jacqui caught her breath. Had Andrea guessed the truth? Before she could speak, Andrea went on:

'To use a ghastly old cliché, Jacqui, I'm walking where angels fear to tread, but are you sure—quite, quite sure—that you really love . . . really love Danny?'

Jacqui's body relaxed. The danger was over! 'I don't know why you and Alain dislike Danny so much. I think he's wonderful, both as a man and as a doctor.'

'We don't dislike him,' Andrea said hastily. 'On the contrary, Jacqui, he's a fine man, but . . . You do realise that he's a dedicated doctor without a private income? Now, this may not seem important to you, but Danny has some . . . well, you could call them 'grandiose schemes'. He has great plans for our part of the continent, Jacqui. He wants a bigger flying doctor service, more clinics with Sisters or male aides in charge who could handle many of the trivial problems that waste his time. He wants more hospitals. A lot of his own money will be spent on this, and if he marries . . .'

Andrea smiled. 'I know you're young and romantic, Jacqui,' she went on, 'but life out here can be very tough. Danny's wife will always have to take second place, for his work will come first.'

'I'm sure if his wife really loved him she'd understand.'

'But how can you be sure you love him, Jacqui? After all, you've only met him about . . . what? A dozen times? To know a man, you need to be in the same house, meeting at meals, early morning, late at night, seeing if he's good-tempered and . . .'

'Surely if you love someone . . . Look, Andrea, I do . . .' Jacqui began, but Andrea hurried on.

'Have you thought it could be unfair to Danny? I mean a wife without a private income of her own, one who isn't even a nurse, and certainly not used to the lonely life you'd lead, for Danny is rarely at home.'

Jacqui drew a deep breath. She was beginning to feel hemmed in—as if Alain and Andrea were determined to marry her off to Danny.

'How . . . what made you think Danny and I are in love? I suppose Alain . . .'

'Yes, he's very upset about it, Jacqui. He feels responsible for your welfare.' Andrea laughed ruefully. 'Gosh, how stuffy that sounds, but you know what I mean. Alain takes these things seriously and he feels that you're in his care. He doesn't feel you would be happy married to Danny.'

Jacqui pursed her mouth. 'Isn't that our business? Or mine?'

'Of course, but you're so young. We've known Danny . . .'

Jacqui sat upright, swinging her legs down. 'What is it you and Alain have against Danny? You're always friendly enough when you see him.'

Andrea coloured. 'Of course I like Danny. We all do, but it's just that I don't think he's the right man for you.'

'Don't you mean I'm not the right girl for him? Just because I haven't any money. All you think of is money! Why don't you marry him, then? With all your wealth, Danny's dreams could come true.'

'Me?' Andrea's cheeks went even redder.

'Of course, I forgot, your parents decided that you should marry Alain. His mother told me that. What I can't understand is that Alain is doing what he was told to do. It doesn't seem like him.'

'Of course he wouldn't. You ought to know

that, Jacqui. When Alain marries, it will be because he's in love.'

Jacqui closed her eyes, because it hurt. Alain loves Andrea. Alain will always love Andrea. Alain will marry Andrea when it suits him. The pain made her say words that later she was ashamed to remember.

'I forgot, Andrea, *you* can only marry a wealthy man in case he's after your money.'

She heard Andrea give a little gasp and opened her eyes. Andrea was trying to smile. *'Touché!'* he said. 'My parents drummed it into me, and it's a horrible thought, that someone you love only wants your money.'

'But surely, if you really loved him, you could trust him?'

Andrea turned away so that Jacqui couldn't see her face.

'There's also another side to the problem, Jacqui. A poor man may love a rich girl and if he's sensitive he might find it impossible to ask her to marry him just because of her money.'

'But if he really loved her and not her money . . . Jacqui began; then Gaynor came running.

'Tucker's up!' he shouted.

Andrea stood up. She smiled. 'I hope I haven't seemed interfering, Jacqui, but we do want you to be happy.'

Walking back to the homestead, Jacqui wondered if Andrea had used the Royal 'we', or if she automatically said 'we' because of the

211

understanding between herself and Alain.

Cool drinks were waiting for them and Alain was there, joking with the children. He looked up, his eyes enquiring, as Jacqui and Andrea joined him, but Jacqui looked away to avoid seeing the smile he would give Andrea.

It was two days later that Jacqui saw the cloud on the horizon. Used to the cloudless blue sky, she was startled. Later in the day, she was even more surprised. She was with the children on the verandah when they heard a strange sound. They looked through the screened windows and saw a number of kangaroos and wallabies jumping by, heads bent forward, paws clasped in front, as they leapt spectacularly over the yellow stubble. There were even a few emus with them with their long necks and enquiring eyes as they looked this way and that and ran in their odd way.

'I wonder what it means.'

Cousin Adela joined them. 'Trouble, that's what it means. Probably a big fire somewhere, Jacqui.'

'There's a cloud on the horizon,' Jacqui pointed out.

The little old lady frowned. 'It doesn't look like smoke to me.'

They saw suddenly that the quiet air-strip with the helicopter and planes resting there was alive with people. The mechanics were pushing the planes to the hangars, everyone

212

seemed to be hurrying about.

Ruggles came to the homestead, his leathery face concerned. 'There's a dust storm coming,' he told them.

'The boss says to put up the shutters and stay indoors. Better shut all the windows, Miss Jacqui.'

Jacqui obeyed, and saw Ruggles and several abos in their brightly-coloured shirts and khaki trousers, with their wide-brimmed hats pushed back on their heads, as they put up the shutters. The house began to be dark, but there were cracks through which they could peep.

The kangaroos had gone. The dark clouds seemed to be filling the sky and approaching with incredible speed.

Already Jacqui could feel tiny pricks on her skin as if some of the dust had gone ahead.

Suddenly there was a strange roar and everything seemed to be red as the dust enveloped them like a London fog, only infinitely worse for the dust, sharp and bitter, penetrated every crack, clinging to their faces, getting into their eyes, their noses and mouths.

Cousin Adela took charge and made them put damp handkerchiefs over their noses and mouths and dark glasses on. She also made them gargle regularly as their throats became dry.

As suddenly as it had begun the dust cloud passed, leaving behind it inches of dark red dust—dust everywhere. Cousin Adela was grumbling about the extra work as everyone gave a hand, sweeping up the dust, sneezing, coughing, their eyes smarting.

Alain came up to the homestead to see if they were all right. He smiled at Jacqui, who was sneezing, and whose throat was sore.

'You see, Jacqui, it isn't all honey and roses living in the Outback.'

His tolerant, almost complacent, she thought angrily, voice riled her.

She lifted her chin and looked at him. 'I never said it was, Alain. If everything was perfect, life would be too boring!'

CHAPTER TEN

It was as if the dust storm brought an army of germs, for afterwards everyone fell ill. Sally was the first to go to bed, sick and feverish, then Gaynor, finally even Cousin Adela collapsed.

As Jacqui stood by the bedside of the indomitable old woman with her flushed cheeks and damp face, she felt sorry for her, sorrier for her than for the others, for it meant a lot to Adela Hollington to have to admit she was 'ill'.

'I'll be all right, Jacqui.'

Jacqui shook her head. 'Look, you know

you're not all right. Just flop and I'll see what Danny says.'

'But how will you manage?'

Jacqui smiled. 'I will. You'll see!'

Later, Jacqui thought, it was easier to *talk* than to *do*. She got on the air to ask Danny and found that the dust storm seemed to have left an epidemic in its wake. Like a swathe of cut grass, it had left its victims behind.

Danny sounded tired when he spoke. 'Look, please don't send for me unless it's a real emergency,' he asked them all. 'I'm up to my eyes and I have to work on priorities. Blood tests are being made and soon we should know what the trouble is, but for the moment . . .' Then he gave them directions as to what to do, and the numbers of medicines or tablets to be found in the first aid box.

Jacqui soon found that quite a few of the men were ill and two of the jackaroos. She organised those who were well as nurse-aides and also some of the aboriginal women, but most of the work fell on her. Fortunately she was well, but as the days passed, she grew more and more exhausted.

When the children were over the worst, their temperatures almost normal, the dreadful bouts of sweating and then being cold had passed, Jacqui put them in the same room so that they could talk to one another. Both looked white and much thinner. Cousin Adela spent most of her time asleep. When

215

she was awake Jacqui sought her advice as she found this gave the old lady a feeling of being necessary. She knew that the ultimate horror in punishment for poor Cousin Adela would be to learn that they could manage without her.

It was about the seventh day that Alain fell ill.

'How can you manage, Jacqui?' he said as he lay in bed, his face grey and drawn. 'Get hold of Danny and ask for a nurse.'

'I'll do that,' Jacqui promised, knowing full well that there wasn't a nurse or doctor available for a thousand miles.

Every day she listened to the medical session and she knew that Andrea, too, was ill. Family after family were reporting that they 'all had it', and obviously Danny was lucky if he got two hours' sleep out of every twenty-four.

One thing, she thought, as she dragged her tired body round, her head aching, maybe now Alain would realise she was not a 'child'. Not that the thought brought much comfort. Every time she went to see if he needed anything, he would ask what news there was of Andrea. It was always Andrea who was in his thoughts.

Eventually, slowly things began to improve. Sally and Gaynor needed little attention, both happily engaged in writing long letters to their parents. Even Cousin Adela was able to sit up and eat ordinary food instead of the horrible-looking 'gruel' she said was the best 'cure'. Alain was still weak and exhausted.

Jacqui stood in the doorway to his room, leaning against the doorpost. How young he looked as he lay under the thin sheet, his eyes closed, she thought; it seemed strange that a strong man like Alain could fall prey to a germ and yet the so-called delicate Jacqui survive! Had she immunity? She wondered. Perhaps this was a germ they often got in England but rarely in Australia.

She yawned. Her whole body ached. The heat of the day was surprisingly high and she went to her bedroom for a few minutes' 'flop'. She had opened the windows earlier. Now she saw that she had left open the screens. Annoyed with herself, for mosquitoes loved to come in and hide until the night hours when they would descend on her ferociously, she walked to the bed and sat down, yawning, stretching her tired limbs. Everything that had to be done was done. For at least two hours and . . .

She stiffened. Sliding with graceful but hideous ease along the floor was a snake.

It was a long snake, with strange markings, looking at her, its head lifted, moving rhythmically from side to side.

Later, she realised, she must have acted instinctively, for suddenly she found herself standing on her bed, screaming . . .

The snake moved nearer, not hurrying, just

taking its time. Jacqui stared, as if mesmerised, at that frightening swaying of the ugly, threatening head.

The door opened. Jacqui could not look away from the snake—she felt rather like a rabbit, gazing fatally into his enemy's eyes.

'Don't move,' Alain said crisply. 'I'll be back.'

He was only gone a few seconds, but it was the longest time Jacqui had ever waited. Somehow she forced herself to stand still, hardly breathing . . .

Then she heard Alain's running footsteps . . . the next moment there was a shattering roar and the snake reared up in the air, frenziedly thrashing his head around before collapsing suddenly on the floor, twitching for a moment and then lying still.

'Jacqui!' said Alain.

She turned and saw him standing there. Literally she fell into his arms, for suddenly her legs were like jelly and she hardly knew what she was doing. She clung to him, still shivering from shock, glad of his arms so tightly round her.

'Are you all right?'

Jacqui nodded. 'Just . . . just dizzy . . .' She managed to gain control and moved away from him, looking up apologetically. 'I'm sorry I screamed like that. I lost my head.'

'I'm not. I might not have heard you if you hadn't screamed and then we'd have lost you.'

He looked round the room. 'Ah, Jacqui, you forgot the screens!'

'I know . . . it was so hot, and I was in a hurry.'

He put his hand gently on her mouth. 'You don't have to apologise or explain, Jacqui. You've been doing a super job and you're just exhausted. I'm getting us a nurse right away. I managed to get one for Andrea as she was all on her own, but if you don't get help soon you're going to crack.'

'The snake!' Jacqui looked at the still coiled horror.

'Get one of the men to move it out. How's Ruggles, by the way?'

'Better. He had it lightly, so he may get up tomorrow.'

Alain put his hands on her shoulders. 'Tell me, Jacqui, how on earth have you managed?'

She smiled. Some of the shakiness was leaving her now, as life returned to normal again. 'The men and boys have helped—we've all . . .'

'Mucked in, so as to speak. A real Aussie undertaking!'

Jacqui's cheeks were hot. 'Not only Aussie,' she said stiffly. 'In England we help one another, too.'

He looked down at her thoughtfully, but in his eyes she could see amusement. He still did not take her seriously.

'You don't say!' was all he said, but as his

hands left her shoulders and he turned away, she knew that it had made no difference at all, he still saw her as a child.

*   *   *

How Alain managed it, Jacqui never knew, but within a few days a nurse flew in with Danny, a big noisy-voiced woman with gentle hands and an air of authority, who soon had Cousin Adela doing what she was told, and the children out of bed. Nurse Bridget Evans arrived at the right moment, because suddenly it was Jacqui who was the patient. It was just as if, now she was no longer needed, Jacqui collapsed. Before she had had no choice, now when there was someone to take over, she felt like a balloon, pricked with a pin and thankfully deflating.

Jacqui lay in bed, sleeping a lot, when awake feeling sick and depressed. Sometimes when no one was around, she wept. She found it difficult not to, for suddenly her future made a doleful picture. Not nineteen yet, but she loved a man who saw her as a child. What sort of future was that? Feeling as she did she knew she would never forget him, that no one would ever be able to take his place in her life. Yet somehow—somehow or other—she would have to leave Kiah station, pick up the pieces of her life and put them together, and make a fresh start. Feeling weak and depressed, she was sure she could never make it. She just wished she could sink into a deep sleep and never wake up again.

Hers was a long, slow convalescence. Danny visited her several times and showed his anxiety because she was not recovering faster.

'You're not even trying!' he accused her once.

Jacqui felt herself blush. 'I'm sorry, Danny, but . . . but somehow I feel life just isn't worth living. I've got no one . . . no one at all, and . . .'

Danny put his hand over hers and she felt the warmth seep into her fingers. 'Is it Alain?' he asked gently.

She looked at him, her eyes filling with tears as she nodded silently.

'I guessed so when Andrea began to talk about you to me. She's got the idea that you love me.'

'I'm sorry, Danny, but . . . but Alain thought I loved you, so I let him think it so that . . .'

'He shouldn't know that you love him?' Danny finished. He sat back, crossing his legs, smiling at her. 'Poor Jacqui! It hurts, the first time, doesn't it? And the second and the last,' he added, an unusual note of bitterness in his voice.

'You won't let them know the truth?'

'Them?'

'Yes, Danny, them! Andrea and Alain. You see, when we went down to Sydney, I met

Alain's mother and she told me that Alain and Andrea were going to be married. I felt sure Alain wouldn't marry Andrea just for her money . . . I mean, because she is rich, though that was how his mother made me feel. I'm sure Alain would only marry her if he loved her.'

Danny stood up, began collecting his stethoscope and other things. 'I'm sure Alain will only marry Andrea if he loves her—but who could help loving her?'

At the door, he turned. 'Make a big effort, Jacqui, and get up tomorrow. It's the first effort that's the worst. Afterwards you'll feel strength flowing back into your limbs. Physically, there's nothing wrong with you. Promise?'

'I promise,' she said.

She kept her promise the next day. A plane had just flown up from one of Alain's citrus orchards in Queensland. It also brought the mail. Jacqui had two letters, one from Mrs. Plaister with news that her husband was going to retire the following year.

'Not from choice, my dear, but his health isn't so good. I .don't know where we'll go. I'm glad you're so happy,' she wrote.

The other was from Kay Dunn. 'We've got a lovely little house with a spare bedroom, so come when you like, but I'd suggest you see as much as you can of Australia first.'

Sally was reading a letter she had. The

convalescent patients were all on the balcony, with Nurse Evans fussing happily around. Suddenly Sally dropped the letter, her face radiant.

'Jacqui, Mummy says Daddy's got to stay in England for six months for . . . for observation, I think it was, and he wants us to fly over at once to be with them! Gaynor, d'you hear that?' Sally's eyes were shining with happiness. 'Oh, isn't it fab? Flying to England, and Dad's going to take us on a tour, and we're going to . . .' She stopped speaking and looked at Jacqui. 'Mummy says would you fly back with us and she'll pay your return fare. Oh, you will, Jacqui, you will, won't you?'

Jacqui sat very still. So the end had come, far sooner than she had expected. She looked round her. Alain had put down his letters and was staring at her oddly. Cousin Adela had a smug sort of look as if glad to get rid of the Pommie who had proved capable of running the homestead. Gaynor's eyes were full of appeal and Sally was smiling delightedly as if she knew Jacqui could not refuse.

*   *   *

Suddenly everything began to happen. The excitement, bred by the children's eagerness to go to England and their parents, vibrated over the Galah session, with everyone urging Jacqui to come back one day, wishing her luck, giving her endless messages to give to friends or relatives in England.

Danny came out to see them and refused to let them travel for two weeks. They were none of them well enough to risk the exhaustion of a long flight, he said. Jacqui wondered if that was the *real* reason or if he said it to give her a little longer to be with Alain. If Danny had done it out of kindness it misfired, for every day spent near Alain made her feel more unhappy.

Alain showed no signs of minding they were going. He had said it would be better for the children to be with their mother. He had told her the salary he was paying her and she knew it was generous enough to let her tour Australia if she flew back. But now she was wondering if she would come back. Australia had too many painful memories. If she was to get over her love for Alain, surely it was better to stay twelve thousand miles away? If she liked, she could go to Canada and build a new life there—there was no reason why she should come back to Australia. No reason at all.

Except the fact that she loved Australia and that the man she loved lived there.

Each day that passed increased her misery. Was this love? she wondered unhappily; that highly-praised emotion called love. This awful desolate emptiness that filled her. The torture of being in a room with him while he treated her as he treated Sally . . . with that kind, friendly, almost condescending manner.

She was not a child. Sometimes she wanted to scream at him:

'I'm a woman . . . a woman . . . a woman!'

Of course she didn't. She moved round, smiling fixedly, saying goodbye during the Galah session to her friends, spending a day with Andrea, who was taking longer to recover than anyone, and who looked pale and frail. They talked while Alain, who had flown Jacqui over, went round the station to check up on things.

'And you and Danny?' Andrea asked, looking as beautiful as ever, her frail look seeming to increase her beauty, if that was possible.

Jacqui shrugged. 'There's no hurry for that.'

'You're coming back, of course?' Andrea's voice was anxious.

Jacqui went over to the window. She could see the blue mountains in the distance, the clumps of eucalyptus gums, probably occupied by koala bears, she saw a group of kangaroos by a stream that had once been full of water but was now caked with sunbaked dirt.

'I don't know,' she said over her shoulder. 'I just don't know.'

And then came the last day, a long emotional day which never seemed to end. Farewells on the Galah sessions, then visits to the abo men and women she had grown to know, the children clinging to their mothers' long skirts, their faces scared as they stared at Jacqui. The final packing, listening to the children's excited voices and a last look round. Jacqui stared at the small clump of ghost trees. Their silver-white trunks and strangely grotesque gestures seemed to fit her mood perfectly.

One day this would be Andrea's home. She and Alain would have children who raced out there in the sunshine, laughing, singing. And those trees would still be there . . .

She turned away quickly to meet Cousin Adela's grave gaze.

'Come back to us, Jacqui,' the old lady said quietly. 'We've grown fond of you, for you're a beaut girl, you know.'

Jacqui's eyes filled with tears. For one awful moment, she thought she was going to break down.

'Thanks!' Instinctively she put her arms round the little old lady and hugged her. 'I'll miss you, too,' she gasped, and hurried out to the waiting car where Ruggles was at the wheel.

The children were in the car already, waving happily to Cousin Adela who stood still, watching them drive away.

Alain flew with them down to Sydney. The children were too excited to think about feeling air-sick. For once it was Jacqui who looked green and was given a pill by Alain to swallow.

'I didn't know you got like this,' he said, 'or I'd given you a pill beforehand.'

Just as he would have given one to Sally, had she needed it, Jacqui thought unhappily.

'I don't usually,' she managed to say.

He frowned. 'I'm not sure you ought to be flying so soon. You still look pretty weak.'

'I'll be all right . . . she said, and opened her book, pretending to read. Of course she'd be all right! She had no choice.

*   *   *

They spent two days in Sydney, Alain taking the children to see his mother, Jacqui pleading a headache that didn't exist. And then came the final day.

Alain went with them to the airport, Ruggles was looking after the luggage.

There was a cold wind blowing across the tarmac. The huge plane stood there, immaculately massive. Jacqui looked at it and swallowed. This was the end.

She turned round to look at Alain and held out her hand.

'Goodbye.'

'I'll see you on board,' he said.

They went up the gangway into the plane, the pretty blonde hostess showing them their seats.

Alain sat down by Jacqui, talking about the children and their excitement. 'What

227

a difference it's made to Sally,' Alain said, looking across the aisle to where Sally and her brother were arguing happily. 'You did us a lot of good, Jacqui.'

Jacqui stared at him. Would she ever forget him? She wondered. Inside her something seemed to curl up and die. Did she want to forget him when he meant so much to her?

She heard a voice telling them to do up their safety belts.

'You ought to go,' she said to Alain quickly.

He smiled and did up his safety belt. 'I'm coming with you.'

'You're . . . you're *what?*'

He smiled again. 'Coming with you.'

'But. . .' Why was he coming? Because he wanted to go to England? But then he could have taken the children and left her in Australia. 'I don't understand.'

His hand closed over hers tightly. 'So that I can make sure you come back to Kiah.'

'You . . . you want me to . . .?'

She could hardly speak. She couldn't understand what was happening. She couldn't believe it when he took a small box out of his pocket, opened it and showed her, lying on a velvet background, the most beautiful ring she had ever seen.

It was an emerald—a large oval emerald, with a border of tiny diamonds.

Jacqui looked up at his face. 'I just don't understand . . .' Vaguely she knew they had taken off, were climbing high above the clouds.

'I thought we'd go and meet your nice Vicar's wife, Mrs. Plaister, and I'll ask for your hand in marriage,' Alain said, his voice casual. Just as if he was suggesting a picnic by the creek!

'Hand in marriage?' Jacqui whispered.

Alain looked surprised. 'Something wrong, Jacqui? It's not like you to echo my words.'

'But . . .'

'You were so sure I was in love with Andrea, weren't you?'

'Aren't you?'

He smiled. 'Most certainly not. I love her, yes, but that's quite different. I've known her since she was a child.'

'But your mother said . . .'

'I know. Poor Mother, don't blame her too much. You see, she came from a very poor family and can still remember the horrors of 1933. She can't believe that we're secure financially, as secure as it's humanly possible to be. That's why she's so obsessed with the idea of my marrying Andrea. We never took it seriously. It was a sort of family joke.'

'But I thought Andrea . . . I'm sure she loves you.'

Alain laughed gently and took her hand in his. Her left hand.

'Jacqui, for once you're way out. Andrea's been in love with Danny for years. He's in love with her, but he won't ask her to be his wife.

He's proud. She's wealthy.'

'Andrea . . . and Danny?' Jacqui repeated softly. She was beginning to understand many things—Andrea's distress and concern about Jacqui loving Danny.

'Yes. I had a few words with Danny. I felt he was going too far and I told him so. Wrecking two people's lives just because he's too proud to marry a woman with more money than he has. We exchanged views.' His hand tightened round hers. 'I . . . I was pleased by some of the things he told me.' He glanced at his watch. 'About now, Danny will be at Andrea's. He was going to take the clinic there. He said he'd pop the question, and I know what Andrea will say.'

'I'm so glad for them!'

'So am I. Jacqui, is it true? Do you love me?'

She turned in her seat to look at him. 'Of course I do.'

'I couldn't believe it. I'd seen you as a child . . . it wasn't until you nursed the lot of us like a valiant Florence Nightingale that I realised you were a woman . . . but I think what finalised it was when the snake frightened you so much. You were in my arms, clinging to me like a frightened child. I knew then, for sure, that you were the only woman I would ever want to marry. May I?' he asked, sliding the ring on her finger.

It fitted perfectly. 'Oh, Alain!' was all Jacqui

could say.

Gaynor came across the aisle, his face green. 'I think I'm going to be sick, Jacqui.'

Alain laughed. 'Oh, no, you're not, young man! Go and tell Sally that Jacqui and I are going to be married.'

'You are!' Gaynor's face changed, lost the green look as his eyes brightened. 'Good-oh! Then she'll be our real auntie!'

He turned across the aisle, his voice loud and clear.

'Uncle Alain's going to marry Jacqui, Sally!'

'Fab . . . absolutely fab!' Sally shouted, waving her hand. 'Oh, Jacqui, now you'll live at Kiah and you'll always have those ghost trees that fascinate you so much.'

Jacqui nodded happily. Yes, she would live at Kiah, with the ghost trees she loved. And of course, with Alain, the man she loved, too!